28193

Fisher, Earl G.

A Slug of Hot Lead

DATE DUE

AG 12 '02			638
OC 28 '02			

Bourcey. 11.72 1-15-02 5D

A SLUG
OF
HOT LEAD

A SLUG
OF
HOT LEAD

•

Earl G. Fisher

AVALON BOOKS
NEW YORK

PRINTED IN THE UNITED STATES OF AMERICA
ON ACID-FREE PAPER
BY HADDON CRAFTSMEN, BLOOMSBURG, PENNSYLVANIA

To my loving wife, Linda,
who helps me remember not to ever give up.

Chapter One

J oe Weaver, the recently hired foreman of the Summerlin ranch, stood inside Pettigrew's Provisions, talking with the store's owner, Paul Pettigrew. Standing beside Joe was Chili, his second-in-command, who was also the ranch cook. They had made the two-day journey so they could stock up on provisions. Not only did they need such items as flour, cornmeal, and oats for the running of the ranch, but they also made the trip in order to provide horse and cattle feed to get them through the long winter ahead.

"Are we in agreement, then?" Joe asked Paul Pettigrew, who was one of the largest handlers of stock feed in Colorado. "Will you do it?"

"It's hard to trust a man solely on his handshake anymore, Joe," Mr. Pettigrew said. "The fact that you work for Missus Summerlin helps, but she's not the one here making the deal. You are."

1

Paul Pettigrew looked Joe squarely in the eyes the entire time he talked with him, and Joe never let his own gaze falter.

Mr. Pettigrew narrowed his eyes. "You're kind of young to manage a ranch, aren't you, Joe? That's one tough job nowadays."

"I'm twenty-two, Mister Pettigrew, but I've got a lot of experience handling stock and men. I joined the Army when I was sixteen and served five years as a tracker, guide, and a translator. When I got out of the Army, I continued to work for them as a provisioner, among other things."

"No wonder you drive such a hard bargain," Mr. Pettigrew said.

"Joe has done much more than what he just told you, Señor Pettigrew," Chili said, touching the brim of his huge sombrero. "Not only did he save my life, he's the one who busted up the Sutch gang, all by himself!"

"Not quite by myself, Chili," Joe said with a grin. "I couldn't have done it alone. Without you and Flap Jack, I'd be vulture bait right about now."

"If Joe says he will honor the agreement, Señor Pettigrew," Chili said, "he will do it. Joe may seem young, but he knows what it means to give his word. Once given, he will keep it."

Mr. Pettigrew grinned and reached for Joe's hand. "Then the answer is yes," he said. "We have a deal. I'll provide you with enough oats and timothy hay to feed your cattle and horses through the winter. In return, you'll bring me eight head of cattle, four heifers and four bulls, by next May first."

Joe smiled broadly and shook Pettigrew's hand with genuine warmth. Bargaining with the man had been difficult because Joe did not have hard cash to pay for the provisions. He considered himself fortunate that Mr. Pettigrew would trade with him. If Mr. Pettigrew was willing to deal based solely on Joe's word, he knew he would have to keep his word or the man would never trust him again.

"I appreciate your help, Mister Pettigrew. Without you, we'd have had a rough winter ahead. Now we can rest easy. And don't worry about your cattle. They'll arrive on time, fat and ready to go to market. Chili and I will bring them through Cottonwood Pass personally!"

Mr. Pettigrew suddenly stiffened. "Your ranch, the Summerlin place, is up past Cottonwood Pass?"

"Yep. Wonderful country up there. You know it?"

"Been there a time or two, but that's not why I'm asking. You do know what the word is, don't you? About what's going on up there?"

"No. What do you mean?" A chill ran up Joe's spine. He pictured his sweetheart, Emma Summerlin, and a nagging fear crept up his back with the chill. Emma was the main reason he had taken the job as foreman for Mrs. Summerlin. He wanted to be near Emma as much as he could, and working on the ranch was perfect. The thought of her being in danger worried Joe more than he would have imagined.

"There's a gang of horse and cattle thieves operating in the state," Pettigrew said. "It's said they passed through the southern plains about a week ago, heading north."

"If they headed north from anywhere around here," Joe said cautiously, "they would pretty much have to go right through the Summerlin ranch. You sure about this?"

"I'm just telling you what I heard, Joe. The marshal's got a posse going after them, and that's what he told me several days ago. He also said these guys are mean. Mean and no-account. They settle all their differences in one way, and only one way—with a slug of pure, hot lead!"

"If you'll excuse me, Mister Pettigrew, Chili and I have a hard ride ahead of us." Joe touched the brim of his Stetson and turned to Chili.

"If we ride all day and all night, we might get there in time, Chili. Are you ready and willing?"

Chili hoisted a bushel bag of oats in each arm and started toward the door.

"I'm way ahead of you, Joe. Let's load up the wagon and ride!"

Tommy Summerlin was only ten years old, but tonight he felt much older, as if he were at least fifteen.

The moon was half full, casting a pale yellow glow over the landscape. It was just enough light to enable Tommy to see as he ran from a cottonwood to a spruce, making sure he was hidden from sight while he sneaked up on the drovers. The men had encamped a mile from the ranch where Tommy lived with his mother and sister.

Joe's going to be proud of me, Tommy thought as he got close enough to the camp to see the flickering light from the campfire.

Tommy's mother had hired Joe Weaver a few months ago to help run the ranch. His father had died in a gunfight with a gang of bank robbers, and the ranch was too much for Mrs. Summerlin, her daughter, Emma, and Tommy to run efficiently.

Joe had left with the Mexican cook, Chili, two days ago to purchase provisions. It was early September, and still hot on the Colorado plains, but in several months the cold, snow, and sleet would move in, and ranch foremen needed to plan ahead to enable beasts and people to make it through the hard winter.

Yesterday afternoon the drovers had come through, driving a small herd of cattle and horses northward, to Denver, where they told Mrs. Summerlin they planned to sell the stock. There were six of the drovers—sunburned, hardened men who spoke little, kept to themselves, and looked to Tommy more like bank robbers than stock drovers.

Tommy had a feeling, a gut feeling, that something about these men was not quite right. With Joe gone, it was up to him, as man of the house, to make sure the drovers did not take advantage of his mother and sister.

"We need some fresh horses, lady," the leader of the drovers had explained to Mrs. Summerlin. "My name's Colonel Teton. Our family's name is the same as the Wyoming mountain range. I served with honor in the U.S. Army, but now that I'm retired, I enjoy running stock every now and then."

Mrs. Summerlin, unsure what to answer, simply nodded.

"These nags are near-about wore out," Col. Teton said.

"They're still good horses, just a little tired. If you'll swap us six fresh ones for these six, I'll give you two head of cattle for profit. What do you say?"

Mrs. Summerlin had been born and raised on a ranch. She examined the six horses, and agreed with Col. Teton. The horses he rode were good stock, but underfed and over-worked. With rest and food they would be as healthy as her six in a week, plus she would gain two head of cattle in the deal. It was too good to pass up.

"Done," she said.

"Done," he agreed. He did not reach out a hand to shake with her. "We'll be back about two hours after sunrise, ma'am. Will you be up that early? Ready to make the trade?"

"Oh, yes," Mrs. Summerlin said. "We'll be up at sunrise. By the time you get here, we'll have you a good, hearty breakfast ready—steaks, biscuits, and gravy. No charge to you, either. I'll throw that in as part of the deal."

"Much obliged, ma'am." Col. Teton and his men ex-amined the Summerlin horses, about fifteen head, each man picking the one he wanted. Tommy noticed that the men also eyed the fifty head of longhorns that he and Joe had brought in from the range two weeks ago.

"See you in the morning, Missus Summerlin," Col. Teton said, tipping his hat. He turned his horse, and he and the men headed back to their camp.

Tommy had watched the entire affair without saying a word. Joe had taught him that when you wanted to learn about a person, let *him* do all the talking.

"Watch his body speak," Joe had said.

"A body can't speak," Tommy replied. "What are you talking about?"

"Sure it can, Tommy. For instance, pay close attention to a man's eyes—they talk plenty. If a man won't look at you, or if he stares at the ground a lot, there's a good chance he's lying to you."

Joe purposely watched the ground as he talked, to give Tommy an idea of what to look for. "Watch his hands, too. If he keeps them in front of his face, rubbing his chin, scratching his mouth, it might be because he's using his hand like a bandanna, to hide his features."

"Why?"

"That way you can't identify him to the law. It makes it harder to describe him."

So Tommy watched the man who called himself Colonel Teton, and the colonel's body talked plenty. The man was over six feet tall and heavy, about two hundred pounds, Tommy guessed. He kept his tan, sweat-stained Stetson pulled down over his forehead, so Tommy could not tell how much hair he had. He could see wisps of reddish-brown curls sticking out from behind the hat. The man had a full beard, also reddish-brown, that did a much better job hiding his facial features than either a hand or a bandanna could have done. Tommy realized he would never be able to describe the man's chin or mouth, because they could not be seen.

But it was the colonel's eyes that clinched it for Tommy. The entire time he was talking to his mother, Colonel Teton's eyes looked everywhere but on her eyes.

Tommy caught the colonel's glance for a brief moment, and the cold, steel-blue gaze seemed to bore right through him, like a double-barreled shotgun taking aim.

That was when Tommy decided to sneak up on the drovers once night came, and see if he could learn a little more about them.

Joe will be right proud of me, he thought again. *I'm acting just like he would.*

Tommy could see the men's faces now, five of them, as they sat around the campfire. He closed in, creeping up behind a boulder near enough to overhear the men, yet not be seen. He felt for his father's Colt .45, stuck in his belt, just in case he needed it.

"Hoo-haw!" one of the drovers said loudly, laughing at the same time. "*Colonel* Teton, is it? You sure are the high and mighty one today, Teton Tom. *Colonel*? Where the Sam Cactus did you come up with that one? Next thing we know, you'll be telling folks you're a fancy dandy, or such."

"It ain't but half a lie, Hoosegow," Teton Tom said. "If you recall, I was in the Army."

Hoosegow laughed again. "Yeah? You were a lousy private, too. And you deserted after less than a year, taking the real colonel's horse as your departing pay! Hoo-haw! You're a durn good liar, Teton Tom."

"It's no matter," Teton Tom said. "We've got work to begin. You boys ready?"

"Lemme finish these beans," one of the other men said. "If we're gonna steal all the woman's horses and her cattle, too, then ride all night, I got to have some beans in me."

"It's no wonder we call you *Beans,* Beans!" Hoosegow yelled. "I'd heap rather wait till in the morning after a decent breakfast of steaks, biscuits, and gravy, myself."

"Can't wait," Teton Tom said. "That stupid woman and her two brats will be up at the crack of dawn, waiting on us."

"Just two more bites," Beans said.

"By the time she's got food ready," Teton Tom said, "we'll be halfway to Wyoming. Come on. Let's saddle up. I love to steal, but it's hard work."

Tommy's eyes grew as wide as two of his mother's biscuits. *So that's what they're up to*, he thought. The next instant he turned to run back to the house. He knew that if he, his mom, and Emma were armed and waiting, that the rustlers would probably run off without taking a thing. Men like these rarely stayed put for a gun fight, especially at night when they could not be sure who their adversaries were or how many of them they were facing. He needed to get back to the ranch as soon as possible.

Whump!

Tommy ran into something.

"And where in tarnation do you think you're runnin' off to, you little bedbug?" a gruff voice shouted in his ear. Strong arms circled Tommy, pinning his own arms to his sides, as the man hoisted him into the air and marched into the light of the campfire.

"Lookee what I caught!" the man yelled to the others. He pulled Tommy's revolver from his belt and dropped him into a heap on the ground.

"We got us a bedbug, if I ever saw one!" the man shouted. "A *big-eared* bedbug, if you fellers know what I mean. Do you fellers know what we do with bedbugs?"

"Yeah," Teton Tom said, striding toward Tommy. "We crush 'em!" His eyes locked with Tommy's and never wavered for an instant.

Chapter Two

Even though the wagon was loaded down with supplies, Chili drove the two horses, a tan gelding and a pinto mare, as hard as he could without harming them. The gelding, Cortabolsas, was his favorite. When the wagon was to carry only a small load, Chili would hitch up Cortabolsas by himself, and the heavily muscled gelding could usually pull the wagon easily. Chili knew that today's load would be larger than normal, however, so he had hitched both horses to the wagon before they left the ranch.

Joe rode beside the wagon on Davey, his bay stallion. He had named Davey after his younger brother, who still lived in Virginia with his parents. Joe had not seen any of his family for more than five years now, but he was not thinking about them. Instead, his mind was on Emma. He thought about Emma, with her long blond hair tied back in a ponytail. He daydreamed of Emma, who, once she had turned her deep, blue eyes on Joe, captured his heart forever. Joe needed to get back to the Summerlin ranch as fast as possible so he could be sure that Emma was safe and sound.

"Chili!" he called out. "Don't push 'em too hard. We need to pace ourselves, or we won't ever get there at all, much less in time."

"They're doing fine, José. They want to get home as badly as we do, only for different reasons." Chili turned toward Joe and grinned, even though Joe could barely see him in the dark. All Joe could make out was the huge sombrero Chili wore, day and night.

"I promised Cortabolsas and the mare a potato *and* an apple, if we arrived back at the ranch before supper tomorrow. They are as anxious to get home as we are."

"We'll make it, Chili. Davey's holding up fine, and those horses will, too, if we just pace ourselves. Let's don't overtax them."

"Oh, no, José. I will not . . . Ah! Caramba!"

Ka-whump!

The right front wheel of the wagon struck a rock and suddenly disintegrated, throwing Chili, the wagon, and all of its contents high into the air.

With a sickening thud, the wagon slammed down on the hard road, busting the other wheels as it crashed, then skidded along until Chili could bring the horses to a stop.

"Agh!" Chili yelled, hopping out of the wagon to survey the damage. "We are ruined, José. The wagon is destroyed."

Joe reined Davey to a stop beside the wagon, dismounted, and looked at the wreckage, shaking his head sadly.

"What do we do now, José? We can't fix the wagon, and we can't just unhitch the horses and ride off to the ranch. If we do, all the supplies we just bought will be stolen by every Tomás, Ricardo, and Enrique who comes along. We are done for!"

Joe and Chili had taken everything out of the wagon and piled the goods under a canvas cloth to protect them from the drizzling rain.

The horses were nervous, but otherwise were quite content, munching on stray potatoes that had rolled all over the ground from a burst burlap sack.

"We only lost one bushel of potatoes, a few pounds of flour, and one bag of sugar, José." Chili busied himself, picking up the shattered pieces of a salt lick. "I think the cattle will still use this salt lick, even if it is broken, but I do not think Missus Summerlin will want the sugar. It is mixed in with the mud, and will be very difficult to separate."

"Yeah," Joe mumbled. He was picking up loose potatoes and stowing them in a pile next to the wagon, out of range of the two horses. Davey was ground-reined several paces away, and contented himself with watching the goings-on.

"These potatoes are bruised," Joe said, "but still edible. Let's get them picked up before those two horses eat all of them."

Chili grabbed two just as the pinto swung his head toward them.

"What now, José? Should I stay here and guard the wagon while you ride on to the ranch? You could send Tommy back for me in another wagon."

"That would take too long," Joe answered. "This wagon's still in good condition, actually. The axles are almost new and the sideboards are only a year old. All it needs are four new wheels."

"Ay, José. But without proper tools, we cannot make wheels."

"That's true. But let's think about it, Chili. There has to be another way."

"Another way? Impossible!"

Joe laughed. "My dad taught me that there were three ways to do anything, Chili. Three ways! The problem is to think of them."

"Three? You must be loco. The only way to pull a wagon is on wheels."

Joe shook his head. "The Indians move heavy objects all the time, and they don't use wheels."

Chili's eyes opened wide. "Ay! You are correct, José. I have seen them pile their teepees, animal skins, and even old people onto the travois, but it only touches the ground in two small places at the end of two poles. Our wagon touches the ground everywhere!"

"You're right, Chili, but how about sleds? The kind my dad used to make for us in Virginia, that slide over snow."

"There is no snow here, now, José." Chili grinned. "Although I may still be here in December when the snow *does* come. *Then* we could make the wagon into a sled."

"Maybe the mud will be like snow, Chili. If we can remove the axles and just have the wagon supported by the two undercarriage boards running the length, maybe it will slide like a sled."

"Hmm. Only one way to find out, José."

By lifting the corners of the wagon one at a time, and placing them on four oaken casks of gunpowder they had bought at Mr. Pettigrew's, Joe and Chili were able to work on the underside. They removed the axles and the hardware that fastened them to the undercarriage, leaving only the two long boards at the lowest point.

"As wet and slick as this trail is, Chili, I believe our plan will work." Joe grabbed an ax from the pile of dry goods and walked to the front of the wagon. "All we need to do is angle the front edge of the boards, like the leading edge of a sled, so they don't dig into the mud."

Joe whittled down one board and Chili cut the other. They pulled out the casks, one at a time, just as they had done when they raised the wagon, and lowered it to the ground. They loaded all the goods back in the wagon and stared at it, hoping for the best.

"We need to get started as soon as possible," Joe said. "We don't want the wagon sinking into the mud and getting bogged down. We want it to glide across the mud."

"Okay," Chili said. "I'm ready." He took a seat on the wagon and shook the reins. "Gee-up, Cortabolsas! Haw!"

The two horses pulled and pulled, but the wagon barely slid forward, inching its way down the road.

Chili jumped out, still grasping the reins, and ran to the back of the wagon, where he began pushing. Joe joined him, and by pushing together, the wagon began to move faster.

"I must walk beside it, José. My weight adds too much for the horses to manage." He shook the reins again and the horses began pulling the wagon at a fast walk.

"We did it!" Chili shouted. "We'll make it. It'll take me two days at this rate, but we'll get there. You need to go on, José, on to the ranch. They may need your help."

"You sure you'll be okay, Chili?"

"Of course I will." He shook his head from side to side. "One thing I do not know, though."

"Oh? What's that?"

"We have devised a *second* way to move the wagon. What is the *third*?"

Joe frowned. "Don't know, for sure." The rain began falling heavier and he looked up into the dark sky. "But if it rains a bunch more, the wagon may start floating. That would be a third way, wouldn't it?"

"Ay! You are right. And I do not know how to swim. Gee-up, horses! Haw!"

Joe did not wait much longer. He mounted Davey, turned him toward the ranch, and galloped away, losing sight of Chili and the wagon in the darkness in a few seconds.

Joe was worried about Emma. She was on his mind every minute. Emma was on his mind, and fear knotted his stomach.

Chapter Three

Using a trick he learned as a scout in the U.S. Army, Joe and Davey traveled all night long. He never let Davey break out into a full gallop, because that would have worn him out in a few hours. Instead, Joe would let Davey move into a fast trot, a speed that seemed comfortable for the muscular horse, for about twenty minutes. Then he would make Davey walk for twenty minutes.

Joe did not have a watch, and it was nighttime, so he could not use the sun to tell time. Nor could he estimate the passage of twenty minutes by the stars, because the normally star-filled sky was clouded over. Joe was thankful it had stopped raining, but he wished there were stars above that he might use as a watch. Instead, he had to gauge the time by the amount of sweat that formed on the top of Davey's neck. It took about ten minutes for the sweat to form. By the time another ten minutes had gone by Davey was sweating profusely, and Joe would slow him down to a walk. After Davey's neck dried and his breathing had been normal for several minutes, Joe would prod the horse into a trot again.

Using this walk-and-trot method, Joe reached the Summerlin ranch about two hours after sunup. Though he was sleepy and exhausted, Joe knew that Davey was even more so, and he wanted the horse to have food, water, and rest as soon as possible. He was very pleased with the time they had made. It would be after dark tonight before Chili made it in to the ranch.

He let Davey slake his thirst, pulling him from the water trough before he overdrank. Next he led Davey to the barn, where he removed the saddle, giving him a quick brushdown and a pan of oats. Joe knew the first rule of survival in the West was take care of your horse, and he will take care of you.

Joe gave Davey some more water, then ran out of the barn, heading toward the house. He knew Emma and Mrs. Summerlin were up because he could smell the aroma from the steak and biscuits, even out here in the quiet barnyard.

The quiet! Joe stopped and gazed intently toward the corral and the bunkhouse. *It was too quiet!*

He ran to the corral, his heart sinking. The cattle, the horses—they were all gone. One lonely calf stood next to the fence, braying for his mother.

"What's happened, little fellow?" Joe asked the calf, wishing the animal could talk. "Where is everybody?" Chills ran up Joe's spine as he remembered the gang Mr. Pettigrew had warned him about.

"Emma?" he shouted. "Missus Summerlin? Is anyone here?"

He gave the calf a reassuring pat, turned, and ran back to the ranch house. He leaped into the kitchen as fast as he could. On the still-hot stove, four steaks were cooking, slowly burning to crisp blackness.

Joe scowled. The kitchen had been left unattended, empty. There were only two reasons Mrs. Summerlin and Emma would have left food burning on the stove. Either there had been an emergency—or they were taken away by force.

"Emma?" he shouted again. "Emma—where are you?"

The only sound he heard was the lonely calf, braying in the deserted corral.

"Horses approaching!" Joe whispered to himself. He pulled his Colt revolver and ducked behind the opened door.

He let out a sigh of relief when the riders pulled into view. It was Mrs. Summerlin, Emma, and two ranch hands, Jimmy and Billy.

"Emma!" Joe yelled, holstering his weapon as he ran outside. Emma dismounted and Joe swept her in his arms.

"Oh, Emma! I was so worried about you. I—"

Before he could finish, Emma pushed him away and shrugged out of his grasp. "Don't even talk to me, Joe Weaver!" she yelled, tears rolling down the sides of her reddened cheeks. "Because of you, Tommy's gone! Kidnapped! It's all your fault, Joe Weaver!"

Emma turned and ran into the house without another word, slamming the door behind her.

"She's not thinking clearly, Joe," Mrs. Summerlin said. She dismounted, gave him a quick hug, and pointed to the empty corral.

"As you can see, Joe, we've been robbed. Drovers, passing through on their way north, stopped in the north meadow yesterday and asked if they could spend the night. They wanted to swap their tired mounts for fresh horses, throwing in a few head of cattle to sweeten the deal, and I agreed to it."

She shook her head and fought back the tears forming in her eyes.

"I should have known better, Joe. Instead of an honest deal, they came in the night and stole all of our stock— fifty head of cattle and fifteen horses. The only ones they didn't take were the six horses in the bunkhouse corral and one poor, motherless calf."

"They didn't mess with our horses," Billy said, "because Jimmy and I were sacked out in the bunkhouse, and we'd have heard them if they came that close." Billy was younger than Joe, about nineteen, and very thin, but as strong as the barbed wire he was said to resemble. That was where he got his nickname, Barbed Wire Billy.

"Durn varmints, Joe!" Billy shouted. "You give the word, and me and Jimmy and you will head out after those mangy, snake-eyed horned toads. We'll make 'em pay for stealing Tommy and our stock."

"Not so fast, Barbed Wire," Joe said. "Let me get all the

facts first." He turned to Mrs. Summerlin. "Why does Billy think the drovers took Tommy? When did you realize Tommy was missing?"

"It's the only thing we can figure, Joe. Tommy's bed hasn't been slept in—it's made as fresh as it was yesterday morning. If I had been up and awake, he'd have told me where he was going. Since I was asleep, he probably figured he didn't want to bother me. My guess is he had suspicions about the drovers and rode out to check up on them."

"You know how Tommy is," Billy added. "If he thought his momma was being cheated, he'd try to take care of it. His horse was in with ours earlier, at the bunkhouse corral, and it's the only one missing. That's why we think he rode out, possibly to spy on the drovers."

"And we think he got caught," Mrs. Summerlin said. "Otherwise, he'd be home by now. The smell of my steak and biscuits would draw that boy from across the state if he had half a chance. That's why we think he's been captured."

"And the four of you rode off to look for him?" Joe asked. "What did you find?"

"The drovers were supposed to be here for breakfast two hours after sunup," Mrs. Summerlin said. "Emma and I got up at sunrise and started cooking, and about thirty minutes later Jimmy and Billy busted through the door to tell us all the animals were gone—stolen. I ran out to the corral, and sure enough, all but one little calf was gone. He must've been scared and hid out in a corner. In the dark they couldn't see him, so he got left behind."

Mrs. Summerlin began crying at the thought of the motherless calf. "So we all saddled up and rode out to the north meadow, to see if the drovers were still camped there."

"Did you find any signs of Tommy?" Joe asked.

Mrs. Summerlin shook her head. "Nothing," she said. "We could barely tell where the campfire had been. Oh, Joe, I'm so worried about Tommy. He's only ten. He doesn't know how to take care of himself."

"We figure they've only got about a six-hour jump on us," Billy said. "We can still catch 'em, Joe. The stock will slow them down."

"They can still make Denver before we could catch 'em, Billy. They could sell the stock and be on their way again in no time. I think it's best if I go after them alone. There's supposed to be a posse looking for them, too. If I find 'em, I'll get some help and bring 'em in."

"Please try to keep Tommy from getting hurt, Joe," Mrs. Summerlin said. "I just know he's in big trouble."

"Tommy's pretty smart for a kid, Missus Summerlin. And you could be wrong about him, too. Could be, he's just following the drovers. Maybe he just hasn't been able to get away and come tell us yet."

"None of this would have happened, Joe Weaver," Emma's sharp voice sounded from the hallway, "if you'd have been here."

Joe turned and faced the woman he loved, but she was in no mood for niceties.

"If you weren't off traipsing around the countryside with Chili," Emma yelled, "Tommy would still be here! Safe and sound."

"Now, Emma," Mrs. Summerlin said. "We don't know that for sure. Plus, Joe was away on business, trying to purchase enough feed so our stock could make it through the winter."

"Got it, too, Missus Summerlin," Joe said gravely. "Though it's not of much use now."

"He's right, Momma," Emma said. "There are no animals to feed except one poor little calf and six horses, thanks to Joe not being here." She turned to the frying pan on top of the stove. "And speaking of food, Joe Weaver . . ." She held up one of the steaks in front of Joe's face. The one she chose was burned more than any of the others. "Here's your breakfast, Mister."

Emma dropped the steak at Joe's feet, where it bounced off his boots, landing on the floor.

"Uh, thanks, Emma," he said, turning to head for the back door. "I think it's time for me to go."

Chapter Four

J oe packed his saddlebags, cinched the saddle on Davey, and fed the horse a ripe, red apple.

"Sorry to put you back on the trail so soon, buddy," he said to Davey. He spoke in a soothing, calm voice. "We won't go fast, this time. We'll keep to a walk. But we need to leave soon, while the drovers' trail is still easy to follow. If another big rainstorm comes up, we'll be left guessing which path they took."

Joe led Davey to the ranch house, drop-reined him, and went inside the kitchen. Mrs. Summerlin was hard at work, cleaning up the burned steaks and biscuits that had been left unattended when they had all ridden out looking for Tommy and the drovers.

When she saw Joe, Mrs. Summerlin dropped what she was doing and grabbed a large cloth bag off the wash basin.

"The steaks and biscuits that were salvageable are in

here, Joe," she said, handing him the bag. "I had to scrape the burned edges off some of them, but it's all we have that's fit to take on a ride. I hope you don't think too ill of me for the poor provisions."

"They'll do just fine, ma'am. Thanks. This grub will get me going, then I'll live off the land, if need be."

"You be careful, Joe. You hear me? I want Tommy back safely, but we need you here, too. Don't do anything foolish."

"I won't, Missus Summerlin. I'll be back—*with* Tommy."

"I need to tell you, Joe, how much I appreciate what you're doing—going after those men who stole our stock, as well as going off to look for Tommy."

"I know, Mrs. Summerlin. But it's partly my fault. If I'd have been here, Tommy wouldn't be missing."

Mrs. Summerlin shook her head. "That's not true, Joe. It's not your fault. Emma's wrong to blame you. Please don't be upset with her, though. She's just in a tizzy because her brother's missing." She sighed deeply. "It's as much my fault as anyone's, Joe."

Joe shook his head. "Don't worry. I'll find Tommy. I'll be back home in no time, with the cattle, the horses, *and* Tommy. Those horse thieves won't get away with this."

"I'm not worried about the horses and cattle, Joe—just you and Tommy." She turned so that Joe could not see the tears in her eyes. "Do you want me to send Chili after you when he returns? He can catch up to you in a few hours with a fresh mount."

"No, ma'am. He needs to stay here, with you and Emma. I'll be just fine."

Joe turned and walked to the doorway. "I'll be heading north, toward Wyoming and Montana, Missus Summerlin. The weather's warm now, but it's going to turn cold pretty soon. Too soon. I need to find these coyotes, rescue Tommy, and get back to the ranch before the first snowstorm comes through. Mister Pettigrew is going to start delivering feed in thirty days." He tried to smile. "I need to have our cattle back to the ranch in time for their feed, don't I?"

"Just be sure *you* make it back, Joe."

"Yes, ma'am." Joe walked out the door, looking back once, in hopes that Emma had changed her mind about him. *I could sure use a good-luck hug before I leave*, he thought. But Emma did not appear.

Joe mounted up and rode out to the north meadow where the drovers had camped the night before. His experience as a scout in the Army had trained him well in the art of cutting for sign and looking for clues on the trail.

When he arrived at the meadow, he dismounted and slapped his Stetson against his jeans in anger. "Darn varmints!" he said to Davey, rubbing the horse on the neck. "These guys are smart, Davey. Real smart."

Joe walked back and forth, searching the trampled ground for clues. He found none. Even the campfire had been obliterated by the hooves of hundreds of cattle.

"These thieving briar-heads must have driven Missus Summerlin's whole herd through here, Davey. I had hoped that Tommy might leave us a sign—a signal—to show that he was here. I can't find anything, not a scratch in the dirt, nor a scrap of cloth in a branch. He knows how I search for clues, and if he was here, I'll bet he left us something. But now it's gone—trampled to bits. We can't tell for sure if he was here, or where he might be going. Those drovers made certain he couldn't leave a message. They've obliterated everything."

Joe rubbed Davey between his ears, and the horse seemed to be listening.

"I wouldn't say this to Emma or her mother," he went on, "but it may be we'll never find Tommy. *Never!*"

Joe was sure that Tommy would try to leave him a message. If not at the place the drovers camped, then he would signal Joe somewhere along the trail. Joe decided that this left him with no alternative but to follow the drovers and their stolen stock.

He was certain he could catch up to them before they reached Denver, but he kept Davey at a fast walk, intent on searching every square foot for a sign from Tommy. He was not one hundred percent sure Tommy was with the drovers.

"It's not really relevant whether Tommy's with them, anyway, is it Davey?" Joe said, as they rode up a short, rocky incline. The ground was still damp from the previous night's rain, and Joe made sure Davey stepped carefully.

He was in the habit of talking to his horse when no one else was around. Davey was an excellent listener. He never interrupted, criticized, or put Joe's ideas down, no matter how crazy they sounded.

"Those rustlers stole Missus Summerlin's stock, so that's reason enough to go after them, isn't it, Davey?"

When Davey did not reply, Joe understood him to be in agreement.

"Of course, we suspect those rascals have kidnapped Tommy, because that's the most logical place for the boy to be. Right, Davey?"

Davey was silent, concentrating on his hoof placement as they came down the slope they had just topped.

"We'll just keep cutting for sign as we follow those horse thieves. Sooner or later, Tommy will be able to signal us."

A crow flew by, high overhead, cawing raucously.

They walked on for nearly an hour, following the trail left by the herd. Joe talked the entire time, pausing only when a bird or other small animal caught his attention.

"Whoa!" he suddenly shouted, reining back on Davey.

They were in the middle of a small valley, divided nearly in half by a small stream. On the far side of the water were large trees—alders, willows, and cedars. The side Joe rode on was mostly flat, and was cleared, probably by early settlers. The lay of the land offered a good path for wagons and cattle, as well as fresh water nearby. On both far sides, cliffs rose, about thirty feet high. They were steep, and would be difficult to ride up or down, confining most travelers to the cleared area Joe was on. The cleared side had a few bushes, but only the occasional tree.

Ahead of them was a single fir, about as high as the cliff

sides, and hanging from one of the tree's lower branches was a white cotton shirt.

It was a clear sign, if Joe had ever seen one. He glanced around. Nothing moved. He could not see anything in the trees to his left, nor on the cliff's edge to his right. Still, he had the strange feeling that something was wrong.

He knew the shirt was a sign, but it seemed a little too obvious a sign.

"It looks like it's about Tommy's size, Davey." Joe spoke softer than he had before. He did not want anyone to be able to overhear. "But I don't see how Tommy could take it off, hang it up, and not be seen by the drovers."

Joe edged Davey up to the tree and pulled the shirt off the branch. He held it at arm's length, trying to figure if it was Tommy's.

"Sure looks familiar, doesn't it, Davey?"

Click-click!

Joe froze.

He knew that sound by heart. It was the lever of a Winchester .30-.30 carbine as it loaded a bullet and cocked the hammer.

Chapter Five

"**D**on't move, Mister!" a voice called down from the top of the cliffs on Joe's right. "I've got you centered in my sights! Don't give me a reason to see how true they are! If you do, I'll put a slug of hot lead right between your eyes!"

Joe raised his hands, his gaze sweeping the cliffs, until he caught sight of the man behind the voice. All he could see was the man's huge face, hidden behind a bushy, red-tinged beard. The man kept his tan Stetson pulled down low, shading his eyes and hiding his forehead.

As the man stood up, Joe could see that his body was the right size for the face. The man was huge. On either side of him, two other men with drawn revolvers stood up at the same time. Joe gave a sigh of relief when he realized that these two men were of average size. At first he was afraid he had been set upon by a gang of giants.

The men slid down the face of the thirty-foot cliff, one at a time. Two kept their guns on Joe at all times. It would have been comical to Joe to see grown men sliding down a cliff, if it were not for the fact that the guns they held could have gone off accidentally. As soon as each one reached bottom, he would dust himself, aim at Joe, and call out for the next to slide down. The large man with the beard came last. When he dusted himself, he approached Joe, motioning with the lever-action .30-.30 in his hands.

"Off your horse, sodbuster," he ordered.

Joe obeyed.

"Why are you following us?" the large man asked. "Why is that shirt you snatched out of the tree so important to you?"

Joe smiled, hoping to disarm the man. He wiped his forehead with the shirt and tossed it casually on the ground. "This shirt doesn't mean anything to me," he said. "I saw it hanging in the tree, so I grabbed it. It looked like a good sweat rag."

The red-bearded man grinned. "You answered my second question, now answer the first one. Why are you following us?"

"I'm not following you," Joe said, nodding toward the trail he and Davey had been on. "I'm following a herd of cattle. I don't know who they belong to, but I'm going to try and get hired on when I catch up to them."

It sounded plausible to Joe. He hoped it sounded that way to the large man, too.

"You a cowpoke?" the man asked. "Have you rode herd? You know how to cut doggies and rope wandering calves?"

"Yep." Joe nodded. "I've been mending fences for the past month or so. I'm fed up with it. I want to be back on the trail. Say, are you fellows with that herd? Maybe you can put in a word with the trail boss for me."

"I *am* the trail boss," the red-bearded man said, eyeing Joe intently. "Let's go topside of the cliff and talk this over." He turned to one of his partners. "Hoosegow, you lead the way. When you reach the top, we'll let our new cowpoke follow."

"Okay, Tom," Hoosegow said. He holstered his revolver and scrambled up the face of the cliff, taking longer to climb up than he did to slide down. He reached the top, dusted himself once more, and pulled and out his .45 revolver. He aimed the gun on Joe.

"Send him on, Tom," Hoosegow yelled down to the others.

One at a time, Joe, Tom, and the other man made their way up the cliff. Joe was getting a little edgy about having weapons pointed at him the whole time. He slowly lowered his hands, hoping that would let these men know he was not a threat.

"My horse," Joe said to the man called Tom. "I can't leave him down there."

"He'll be fine, cowpoke. You got bigger things to worry about than your horse. You keep your hands in the air, too, till I tell you different."

Joe raised his arms again and glanced around, looking for a way out of this situation. About sixty paces away was an open shed with three horses tied to it. Joe recognized it as the kind used in this area to cover mine shafts. The shed kept rain out of the shaft while men were mining. It also warned riders to stay away from the open mines, which could be ten feet across and a hundred feet deep. At night-time, a man and a horse could disappear down a shaft without a protective shed and never be heard from again.

"Go get us a couple of ropes, Hoosegow," Tom said. "Me and Beans will watch him while you're gone."

Hoosegow jogged to the shed and pulled two lariats off the horses, then ran back to the group, handing the ropes to Teton Tom. Tom tossed a rope in the dirt at Joe's feet, handing the other one to the man he had called Beans.

Beans took the rope and immediately made a noose. He began spinning the rope, causing the noose to grow slightly with each turn.

"Any good cowpoke can handle a rope," Tom said. He pointed to a stunted scrub alder, four feet tall, about ten paces away. "You can rope a bush, can't you? Any cowpoke should be able to rope a durned old bush that ain't even moving."

Beans and Hoosegow laughed.

"Yeah, cowboy," Hoosegow said. "Rope that bush before it kicks you with its nasty hooves!"

"Go on, cowpoke," Beans said. "It'll be a contest, you and me. First one to rope the bush and hog-tie it, wins."

They all laughed again.

Joe picked up the rope and made a loop at one end. His mind raced furiously, trying to find a way out of this. He was a good roper. In fact, he had won contests in roping.

The problem was that he had not practiced any roping in more than a year. He had been so busy running the ranch that he had let his roping skills become rusty. He hoped his arm and mind would react automatically.

"Like I told you," Joe said to Tom. "I've been mending fences for a while now. I'm out of practice."

"Well, let's just see how good you still are," Tom said. "The herd you're following is ours. Could be, if you can rope at all, we'll take you on, hire you. But we need to know if you can rope worth a hoot."

Joe swung the rope around his head several times, and just as he was about to let it go, Hoosegow shot his .45 into the air.

The loop of rope sailed off, landing in the dirt a half-pace from the bush.

The men all laughed and slapped at each other in jest.

"No fair," Joe complained. "I was distracted."

"There's lots of distractions while you're riding herd, cowpoke," Tom said. "Fact is, you missed."

Joe knew the man was right. He should have roped the bush in spite of Hoosegow's attempt to distract him.

"Not much of a bush roper, are you?" Tom said when he was able to stop laughing. "I think you're a bush *whacker*, not a bush *roper*. That's my guess."

Tom aimed the carbine at Joe's eyes, staring intently.

"Look here," Joe said, tiring of this situation. He slowly lowered his arms to his side. "I'm just—"

Joe heard the rope whip through the air, but before he could react, the loop cinched around him and tightened, binding his arms to his side.

"Now that," Tom said, "is what I call *roping*." He turned to Beans.

"Good job, Beans. Finish tying him up, then bring him to the mine shaft. He sure ain't much of a cowpoke. Let's see if he's a miner. Ha!"

Beans tied Joe's hands behind his back, keeping the lasso tight around his chest the whole time. His hands were not bound very tightly, which gave Joe hope that whatever was in store for him, he could still escape.

Beans pulled the rope, and Teton Tom prodded Joe with the carbine until they reached the abandoned mining shaft shed, which was simply a cover made from timbers, eight feet high. There was a wood railing halfway up that ran around three of the sides, the western approach being left open to allow access to the hole. Joe knew that the rail was designed to keep unsuspecting wayfarers from falling down the shaft, but thought it strange that one side would be left open. He guessed that the unlucky traveler coming from the west at night would have to pray he missed the mine entirely.

The shaft was just a hole about eight feet across, dug straight down into the rocky earth. Joe peered into the dark depths, unable to see past twenty feet. He did notice that someone had done an excellent job smoothing out the sides of the hole. There were very few handholds.

"How deep you reckon it is, Hoosegow?" Teton Tom asked.

Hoosegow tossed a rock over the edge, and bent over, listening intently. It made a dull thud when it struck bottom.

"Sixty, seventy feet, I reckon," Hoosegow said. "Deep enough for our purposes."

"Probably had a wooden ladder once," Beans said to Joe. "It rotted and fell down, no doubt. Hope you don't land on it and bust it up even worse! Ha!"

Beans threw his end of the rope around one of the shed's upright timbers, pulling it until the loop around Joe was snugged tight.

"Hey!" Joe said, backing away from the hole. "You guys can't just . . . oof!"

Tom rammed the butt end of the carbine into Joe's stomach, causing him to crumple onto the ground.

As Beans held tightly to the rope, Hoosegow shoved Joe off the lip of the shaft.

"Wha—" Joe said no more. He dangled on the slim rope, about five feet from the opening. Slowly, he felt himself fall lower and lower into the dark mine shaft.

"So long, cowpoke!" Teton Tom called out, laughing loudly. "If you're any good at digging, you might be able to dig your way to China in a couple of years. Ha!"

Joe worked furiously, trying to free his hands as the rope continued to lower him into the hole.

"Hey, cowboy!" Teton Tom yelled down at him. The rope snugged taut, and Joe swung back and forth, about twenty-five feet down.

"I'm afraid we've run out of rope," Teton Tom shouted. "The hole must be seventy feet deep, and we only brought a thirty-foot rope! Sorry!"

Joe heard all three men laughing at Teton Tom's joke.

"Tell you what, cowpoke. We don't want to seem unfair, or mean. So we're gonna leave the rope with *you*. Maybe you can practice and learn to *lasso* your way out of the shaft! Hoo-ha!"

Suddenly, Joe was falling. Beans had let go of the rope.

Joe hoped Teton Tom was wrong about the depth of the shaft.

Chapter Six

W*hump!*

Joe hit the bottom of the shaft, feet first, and immediately bent his legs and rolled forward, so his legs would not take all the shock. This was a technique he had learned busting broncos. If he was thrown off a horse, which was common in bronc-busting, he would roll with the fall to prevent injuries.

He was dazed from the fall, but when his mind could focus clearly again, he realized he was not hurt. He had no broken bones nor bad cuts. None he could see or feel. He had landed on an old timber, probably part of the ladder or a structural beam used in a tunnel, but it had been so rotten that it broke to pieces beneath him.

Just like Beans had said, Joe recalled.

He glanced up at the top of the shaft, and figured it was not as deep as the rustlers had guessed. He estimated it was closer to forty feet deep than sixty. He was very thankful that it was not deep, and that they had not been able to see the bottom. He was not as severely injured as the drovers had probably hoped him to be.

When his eyes adjusted to the dim light, Joe could just barely see his surroundings. There was a large pile of old boards, some with still-sharp sixty-penny nails sticking out of them. Thankfully, most of the boards were in the opposite corner from where Joe had landed.

He could also make out two tunnels, horizontal mine shafts, that led away from this one, the entrance hole. Evidently, the main shaft led down, then the other two went off in the direction of the vein, either gold or silver. Both of the tunnels were caved in, no longer passable. Joe realized the only way out was straight up.

He continued working at the rope binding his hands, as his eyes searched the shaft's sides for hand and foot holds. There were very few. Joe was certain it would be impossible to simply climb up the sides of the shaft.

"Unh . . . unh!"

With a grunt, Joe freed his hands. He rubbed his wrists and pulled the loop off his shoulders. He almost whistled for Davey. This small taste of freedom gave him hope that he could somehow still escape from the mine shaft.

Suddenly a shadow crossed over the light coming from the top of the shaft. Had someone found him? Was it Davey, come to help him?

"Hey!" Joe called out. "Help!"

A face peered over the opening.

Oh, no, Joe thought. It was Teton Tom.

"You need help, cowpoke?" Teton Tom shouted down at him. "What's wrong? Have you got a busted leg or two?"

Joe knew better than to answer the man. If he thought Joe was healthy, he might start shooting into the hole. Joe knew that even though he could see Teton Tom, the man could not see him.

"Well," Teton Tom said after a few moments. "If it's help you want, then it's help you shall receive. Oh, and don't worry none about your horse. We're gonna sell him to the first mule train we come to. Ha! He'll make a fine mule, don't you think?"

Joe shivered. These men were rotten. Worse than he had ever imagined. No one sold a horse to do a mule's work. No one.

"I am known far and wide as a fair man," Teton Tom yelled. "And I don't want it said that I left a cowpoke helpless in the bottom of an abandoned mine shaft. So, because I am a generous person, I'll let you choose, cowboy. Would you like a ladder, or would you prefer a little helper down there? Huh? Which will it be?" Teton Tom laughed.

Joe did not make a sound.

"Okay. *I'll* choose. Here's your little helper," Teton Tom yelled out. "Maybe he will motivate you to *fly* out of that hole! Ha! He'll durn-sure make you move fast, cowpoke! Here he comes!"

Joe saw the shadow of the three-foot-long, rope-like object as it plunged down the shaft toward him.

Uh-oh!

He could hear the snake's rattles as it fell.

Joe knew better than to expect a fair fight from a rattlesnake. Even though the bottom of the shaft was pitch black, the snake would not be blind. He would be able to sense Joe with his tongue. Joe knew that rattlesnakes were excellent hunters at night, when their prey could not see well.

Joe lowered his gaze so his eyes would adjust to the darkness as much as possible in the short time he had before the snake reached him. Joe heard the sickening thud when the snake hit bottom, and immediately began dancing for all he was worth.

He did the Yellow Ribbon Stomp, the Waltz of the Bootjacks, and the Kick-Like-Crazy Square Dance. He jumped and flailed his leather boots everywhere he thought that snake might be.

After three solid minutes of dancing, Joe stopped and took his bearings. He thought he could see the snake, about three paces from him, lying still on the floor of the mine shaft. Not willing to leave his fate to chance, Joe leaped and landed on top of the snake. He stomped four more times.

The snake did not move.

Joe snatched up the creature by the rattles and flung it against the far wall of the shaft, where, amazingly, it stuck to the dirt wall.

Joe could not believe it, so he examined the snake up close. Somehow, the viper's fangs were embedded into the dirt, causing the snake to hang there, like a wall-mounted trophy.

The snake's predicament gave Joe an idea.

He took one of the rotting boards and beat on the other pieces of lumber until he had freed two of the sixty-penny nails. Each spike was a good six inches long.

Taking a nail in each hand, Joe jabbed one in the dirt wall with his right hand, as high above his head as he could reach. The nail sunk enough to allow Joe to pull himself up. He pulled as far as he could, then jabbed the one in his left hand into the dirt. He pulled up with his left hand.

Suddenly, the left nail broke free of the dirt, and Joe fell the two feet back to the floor. His feelings were hurt more than his body. He had only been able to climb up two feet. He was sure he could go higher than that.

Joe took several deep breaths, just like his father had taught him to do when he needed to solve a problem.

He did know one thing—he was not about to give up. Joe never gave up.

He smiled as he remembered a story his father used to tell him when he was a teenager, about the days when he was a baby, just learning how to crawl.

At that time, Joe's favorite toy was a rattle, a small gourd with dried peas inside. His father would place the rattle on a blanket in front of Joe, just out of his reach. Unable to crawl, but wanting the rattle desperately, Joe would squirm, flail his arms, and even flip over, all in an attempt to reach the toy. He always managed to get it.

Every day his father placed the rattle a little further away. By the end of a week, his father told him proudly, Joe could crawl anywhere in the house. He never gave up.

Joe searched through the pile of rotted lumber and found another sixty-penny nail and a three-foot piece of timber that was still sound.

He tied one end of the rope that Teton Tom had so graciously left him to the middle of the timber, and coiled the rope over his left shoulder, leaving both hands free. The timber swung easily, at about waist high.

Joe took the sixty-penny nails, two in his left hand, one in his right, and jabbed the right-hand nail in the dirt wall, once again as high as he could reach. This time he took the timber and gave the nail a good whack, driving it deeper into the dirt.

Now he was certain the nail would not slip out.

Slowly, nail by nail, Joe inched his way up the side of the shaft. He would stick a nail in the dirt, hold on to the other nail with one hand, hit the nail with the timber, then pull up. He would then pull out the lowest nail, and start all over again.

It took Joe nearly an hour to climb twenty feet. He guessed it was about twenty feet, because he was halfway. He had twenty feet to go. To Joe, this was good progress. None of the nails had slipped out, and he had not fallen. He was pleased.

Joe rested a moment, hanging from a loop of the rope he had thrown around the uppermost nail. This lessened the strain on his arm. Both arms were aching from the exertion. He was very, very tired.

Don't give up!

When he was ready to move again, he decided to try a

shortcut. He tied the loose end of the rope around his waist, and pulled up on the nail with his left hand, to free the end with the timber tied to it. He flung the remaining loops of the rope off his shoulder, then took the timber in his right hand.

He threw the timber upward with all his might. At first he was afraid he might wrench the nail out of the dirt, but it held fast. The timber sailed up and over the lip of the mine shaft. Joe was hoping to throw it far enough to snag on the shed railing. He gently pulled on the rope. The timber slipped over the edge and flew down, narrowly missing Joe's head.

Don't give up!

He pulled up on the rope till the timber was in his hands once again. He took a deep breath and tossed the board as hard as he could. Once again the timber flew over the edge of the shaft, but Joe could not tell how far over the edge.

He gently tugged on the rope again, and the timber slipped over the side and flew down, this time smacking him on the shoulder before it went on its way down.

Don't give up!

Joe pulled the rope back up, and once again threw the timber up and away. It landed on the ground outside the shaft, and when Joe tugged on the rope, this time it grew taut. It was snagged on something.

Unwilling to trust the rope entirely, Joe pulled out the lowest nail and jammed it into the dirt above the highest one, gently pulling himself up on the rope.

Using both the rope and the nails, Joe was able to move

up at a much faster rate than before. In fifteen minutes, he reached the top of the mine shaft. He peered over the edge, letting his eyes adjust to the bright sunlight, as well as making sure that none of the drovers were at the top, lying in wait for him.

There was no movement that he could discern. There was no sound.

Joe saw that the timber on the end of the rope had caught the railing well enough for him to fully put his weight on it, and he quickly pulled himself out of the mine shaft.

Joe turned over on his back and rested, eyes closed, rubbing his aching arm muscles. He massaged one arm, then the other, until the sharp pain in the muscles subsided.

He rolled over onto his stomach and jumped to his feet.

"I'm coming after you, Tommy!" he yelled to the heavens. "And you, too, Davey. Both of you. Wait for me. Don't lose faith in me. *I won't give up!*"

Joe rested several more minutes, then began walking toward the cliffs, eager to be back on the trail of the drovers. He slid down the incline, dusted himself, and went to the stream for a drink of water. He lay prone, letting his whole head sink beneath the cool water, drinking heartily until his thirst was slaked.

That done, he stood and whistled as loud as he could for Davey.

Whee-eet!

"Davey! Can you hear me, boy?" he yelled.

Whee-eet!

Joe knew that if Davey was within hearing distance, and not tied up, he would come running.

He began walking up the trail again, continuing to whistle every few minutes as he strode forward. He kept up the shrill calls for nearly thirty minutes, but Davey did not appear. It looked as if the horse thieves had made good on their word to steal the horse.

Joe began walking in earnest, talking out loud to Davey as if the horse could actually hear him. He was so accustomed to talking to Davey when they rode together that speaking out loud now did not seen unusual to him.

"I'm worried about you, old buddy, but don't worry, 'cause I'm gonna find you. And I'm gonna find Tommy, too. Both of you just hang on. Joe's coming."

He felt for his Colt revolver, and was surprised to find that it was still strapped in his holster. He could not understand why the horse thieves had not taken it when they had the chance.

"Those varmints seemed like the kind of men that would steal the boots off a dead man, two minutes before they buried him. Ha! They probably thought that there was no way a cowpoke could *ever* get out of an old, abandoned mine shaft—with a rattlesnake thrown in, to boot! We showed *those* outlaws, didn't we, Davey? I'll make them pay, Davey. I'll catch up to you, Tommy. I can do anything I set my mind to do, and I'm determined to find you both. Just hold on. Just hang in there. Joe's coming."

Joe began using the same formula he had used earlier with Davey, when he wanted to move as fast as possible without becoming overtired. He would walk for a hundred paces, then run for a hundred. Joe knew that his steely determination would settle all scores in the end.

Chapter Seven

W hen the sun slipped behind the nearest mountain, Joe decided to stop and catch up on his sleep. In the distance he heard an explosion.

Wonder what that was, he thought. *Dynamite? Is there a mine ahead?*

The blast seemed to come from due north, in the same direction the trail was leading. Joe guessed it had been about four or five miles off, an easy walk by tomorrow at noon.

He knew there would be food for sale at a working mine, though it might be expensive.

He felt in his pockets. He still had his money, a gold eagle and two silver dollars. It should be enough to provision him for a week, unless the miners had driven up the prices, as often happened in an area where there was a lot of gold or silver being taken out of the ground.

He took a long, refreshing drink of stream water, and found a level, grassy spot beside the water for his bed. He covered his face with the Stetson, to keep flying bugs away from his nose and mouth while he slept.

When Joe awoke, it was still dark, with no hint of the dawn in the eastern sky. He stretched, drank some water, and began his journey once more. He felt refreshed, so he figured he had slept at least six hours, maybe seven. If he had gone to sleep about nine o'clock, it would be nearly four now. The half moon was still visible in the sky, providing more than enough light to follow the trail.

By the time the sun began rising, Joe felt confident he was close to the site of the explosion he had heard the night before.

He was walking up the crest of a hill when an awful sound cut through the air.

Wham!

Joe actually ducked when he first heard the loud noise, not sure at all what it might be. When he reached the top of the hill he stopped and gazed down at a huge mining camp below, proud that his guess had been correct.

Wham!

Below him was a valley that he guessed had once been green. Now it was covered with miner's tents, sheds, and quickly built shacks. It was definitely a boom camp, with men milling about everywhere below him.

At the other end of the valley from where Joe stood, a cavernous tunnel went into the side of a mountain. It was easily twenty feet tall and thirty feet wide, with two sets of railroad tracks leading into it. From the tunnel, the tracks crossed the valley floor nearly a half mile, ending at a gigantic stamp mill.

Wham!

The stamp mill was the cause of the terrible noise he heard every few minutes.

Joe now understood what was happening. Empty ore cars would enter the mine on one set of tracks, be filled up with rock, then come outside and down to the stamp mill. Once at the mill, the rocks would be crushed by the huge, steam-driven stampers. They would then grind the rock into a powder, later separating the gold from the quartz or granite, whichever kind of rock they were milling.

Wham!

Joe noticed a team of two mules pulling a loaded ore cart out of the tunnel, down the rails to the stamp mill. A man walked behind the mules, driving them forward in front of their heavy load by lashing their backs with a leather whip. Joe winced with each crack of the lash on the poor animals' backsides.

Another team came out directly behind the first, pulled by a mule and a horse. As the mule skinner's whip struck the horse, Joe gasped.

Even from this distance, he recognized the unfortunate animal he saw being whipped.

It was Davey.

Furious, Joe drew his .45 and began running toward Davey and the ore cart. He was so angry he tried to yell, but no words came out.

Earl G. Fisher

No one is going to hurt Davey like that! he thought. *No one!*

Suddenly, a rough hand reached out and grabbed Joe's arm, wheeling him to a stop.

"Not so fast, young feller," a voice said. "You ain't gonna win that fight."

Joe pointed his .45 and peered at the man who had been so foolish as to try to stop him. What he saw surprised him. Holding his arm, with no intention of letting go, was an old man, no taller than 5'4". He had a full, gray beard, and was so thin Joe could not believe the strength in his hand, which still clung to Joe's arm like a snake's fangs. Then Joe noticed the man's eyes—they were deep blue, and he could swear they were smiling at him.

Joe could not see any reason for the man to be smiling, but he had to admit that the man's cheery face defused his anger. Joe sullenly holstered his Colt revolver.

As he did so, he noticed for the first time that the hand holding on to his other arm had only a thumb and two fingers. The ring finger and the little finger were missing. Joe was really amazed at the strength the man had in just three digits.

"How do you know I'm heading for a fight?" Joe asked.

"I've been watching you," the old man said, "*and* your eyes, ever since you came over the hill, yonder. I saw you study on the tunnel. I saw you study on the stamp mill. *And* I saw you study on the mule whippers."

He let go of Joe's arm and turned to watch the ore carts as they were pulled toward the mill.

"I saw how your eyes went dark, young feller, as soon as you saw what the whippers did to those poor animals. Makes me as mad as a wet guinea hen, myself, when I see them treat the stock that way. If I had feathers I'd ruffle 'em so much they'd make a windstorm."

He gazed up at Joe, and this time there was no laughter in his eyes. "The only reason I smiled at you, was to show you I meant no harm. But I need to warn you, it doesn't do any good to go down there and complain about the treatment those poor mules and horses get. None at all. And if you go in there with a gun drawn, you'll do nothing but make a good target for the mine bosses' shooters. They've got armed guards all over the place down there, mostly to stop thieves from stealing the gold dust. But they'd just as soon shoot a man as the mule whippers would lash a mule. They'd pick you off like you were a tin can sitting on a fence post. Don't go down among them with a gun drawn."

"There's more to it than me just being angry about the mule skinners," Joe said. "It's personal. I *am* mad about the way they treat the mules, but they've got a horse hitched up to one of those ore carts, and they're whipping *him*, too."

"Horses and mules are all the same to those fools," the old man said. "Horses, mules, *and* miners—they'll whip one and all. I know how you feel. It's a crime to make a horse do a mule's work. I agree."

"It's more than that," Joe said.

"Oh? How?"

"The horse is mine. He was stolen from me yesterday. I

can't leave him down there. He wouldn't leave me to be misused like that, and I can't leave him to that fate."

The old man scratched at his beard, running his fingers through it to straighten out the tangled whiskers.

"I see, young feller. You *do* have plenty of reason to be mad. But you'll need to be patient. You'll need to wait until dark."

Joe looked down at the railway and winced as he watched Davey get lashed again.

"Don't know if I can wait that long," he said.

"It's the only way you'll save him, young feller. The *only* way. If you go charging down there now, in broad daylight, you'll only make a good target for those shooters, and your horse will end up pulling an ore cart till he dies." He peered up at Joe. "They don't feed the mules and horses too good, either, you know. It's cheaper to work 'em to death on little rations than to buy fresh food. At least, that's the way the mine bosses figure it."

Joe shook his head. He still wanted to face the mule skinners down. He wanted to do it now. He could not stand the thought of poor Davey being beaten and driven the whole rest of the day.

"Please do as I suggest, young feller. Together, we can do more than you can by yourself."

"How can *you* help?" Joe asked. "And how do I know I can trust you?"

The man laughed, loud, as if he had not had a good laugh in a long time. He pulled on his beard and peered intently at the tunnel across the valley.

"I'm a powder man," he said. "Or, I guess I should say, I *was* a powder man. I used to be in charge of setting off the charges, the dynamite for the tunnel. Every night, just as it turns dark, they set off a charge at the far end of the tunnel. This breaks out the rocks for the next day's ore carts."

The old man held up his hand with the three fingers on it.

"I lost two of these old friends about a month ago. The rail boss got hold of some one-minute fuses, instead of ten-minute ones, like he was supposed to do. My guess is, he got 'em cheap. Some card shark probably sold him the fuses as ten-minute ones at a discount, and he pocketed the money that was left over that the bosses had given him. Thank goodness, I was setting off a preliminary blast, using just a blasting cap. It went off in my hand before I had half a chance to shake loose of it. If it'd been a cap *and* dynamite, you wouldn't be standing here talking to me, unless I was a ghost."

The old man grinned. "And I ain't no ghost."

"You still set off charges for them?" Joe asked.

"Nope. The rail boss blamed *me* for the accident. Said I didn't know the difference between a one-minute fuse and a ten-minute fuse. Hogwash! He fired me on the spot. I was still bleeding when he pronounced me canned!"

"They treated you like they treat the stock," Joe said.

"You got that right, young feller. I haven't worked a lick since then, neither." He walked over to a tent, and pulled back one flap.

"It ain't much, young man, but it's what I call home now that I ain't got a job or money." He grinned at Joe once more. "But I do have a bunch of explosives. I think we need to wait until dark, then have us some *fireworks*."

Joe nodded.

"My name's Soapy," the old man said. "You can trust me, young feller, because I *owe* those rascals. I'm your man. Welcome to Lost Gulch."

Chapter Eight

"You just need to come on and sit with me a spell," Soapy said to Joe. "Once dark sets in, we'll go to work and release your horse."

"Why wait until dark?" Joe asked. "Won't they still be guarding everything at night? It seems to me that with all the people roaming around, daylight's better."

"Not really. At night, all they worry about guarding is the stores of gold and the entrance to the Lost Gulch mine. They corral the mules and horses and don't pay them any mind. The poor animals are so worn out and tired, the mine bosses feel that anyone would be a fool to try and steal 'em."

"Maybe they're right, Soapy. If the horses and mules are as tired as you say, how are *we* going to get away? No wonder the mine bosses aren't so vigilant."

"You know your own horse, don't you?"

Joe nodded.

"I saw him yesterday, when three strangers brought him in and sold him. Looked like a right strong horse. Am I right?"

Joe nodded again.

"I do believe he can take a hard day's work, even under the lash, then run all night long to get away from that lash. Am I right?"

Joe nodded again, and this time stuck out his hand. "You're right, Soapy. My Davey will ride like the western winds to get away from here, I promise you. My name's Joe Weaver. I'm pleased to make your acquaintance, Soapy."

Soapy grinned broadly and pumped Joe's hand as if he were priming a well.

"The pleasure is mine, Joe. We're gonna show those mine bosses a thing or two, we are. Now, come on in my tent, and let's make plans. Besides, we don't want to attract too much attention by just standing around flapping our jaws."

Soapy's tent was huge. It consisted of a heavy piece of waterproofed canvas, twenty feet long. It was pegged to the ground on the two long sides, running up to a twenty-foot timber, ten feet off the ground. Each side was at least fifteen feet from the cross timber. At the far end was another piece of canvas, sealing off that end, and the entrance had two large pieces that were sewn into the top, thrown back to allow air and men inside. At the closed end, Joe saw several wooden crates and canvas bags, piled four feet off the ground.

Soapy directed Joe to an empty box. "The only chairs I've got, Joe. Have a seat."

Joe sat on the box and Soapy pulled another from the end and took a seat across from him.

"One reason to come in here," Soapy said, "is to get out of hearing range."

"Hearing range?" Joe asked. "Of what?"

"Not what, Joe. Who. We don't want Snake In the Grass to hear what we say."

"Who is Snake In the Grass?"

"A skinny little feller that works for the mine bosses and himself—stealing, lying, and telling the mine bosses any time someone says anything bad or mean about them. If he finds out you're here to get your horse back, he'll tell on you. He's also a thievin' varmint, too. He'll steal a man's gold dust soon as he turns his back to pan a stream. We got to be on the lookout for Snake all the time."

"Are we safe in here? What if he sneaks up beside the tent?"

Soapy laughed. "He won't do that."

"Why not?"

"Because of what you're sittin' on, Joe."

Joe looked at the wooden crate he sat on with new suspicion. "Just what *am* I sitting on, Soapy? It's not just an empty box, is it?"

"Naw. But it's perfectly safe, Joe. Just a little dynamite."

"Dynamite!" Joe yelled, jumping up. "How is that safe?"

"Because *you're* sittin' on the dynamite and *I'm* sittin' on the blasting caps."

"That doesn't sound so safe to me, Soapy." Joe did not sit back down.

"But it is, Joe. Can't set off the dynamite without a cap. Of course, I pass the word around that everything in here is *real* temperamental, so the snakes and varmints don't come around and get too close. It works. As long as we're in here, Snake In the Grass won't mess with us. Once we're outside—we got to keep our eyes and ears open. Because he'll be sniffin' around with his eyes and ears."

Joe paced back and forth. He wasn't that familiar with explosives, but he knew that they deserved respect, and he intended on giving it to them. Especially in Soapy's tent.

"What are you going to do after we get my horse, Soapy?" Joe asked. "Are you going to ride out of here with me? Stay here? What?"

"Don't know yet, Joe. Where are you going?"

"I'm going after those three varmints who sold my horse to the mine bosses. They've got something else—a friend of mine."

"They stole your friend, too?"

"Yes. He's a boy, only ten years old. His name is Tommy. Those buzzards stole his mom's horses and cattle, *and* kidnapped him." Joe took off his Stetson and slapped it against his knee. "I'm going after them, Soapy. I have to do it."

Soapy slapped Joe on the knee in the same place he had swatted the hat, only harder.

"I'm going with you, Joe!" he shouted. "I'm your man!" He paused for a minute, until the stamp mill sent its thunderous roar through the valley, shaking the very ground.

Wham!

"You hear that blasted stamper, Joe?"

Joe nodded. He could barely hear anything else. The constant clap of the mill had been nonstop ever since Joe had been within hearing distance.

"I've been listening to that blasted blam-blam-blam all day, every day, for nearly three months now. I've heard it so much, I don't pay it any attention. Most likely, it's made me half deaf. I've got to get away from it, Joe." He held up his hand with the missing fingers. "The deafening racket, and the mine bosses who just threw me out of a job, Joe. Those are the reasons I'm going with you. That's why I'm your man. I don't like mine bosses, and I don't like men who steal stock and children. I'm going with you, and there's nothing you can do to stop me."

"That's fine with me, Soapy, but how? As you just told me, all the horses and mules will be worn out. Besides, the only horse I saw was Davey. The rest of them looked like mules to me. Are you going to ride a worn-out mule? If you do, they'll catch us, sure as snow comes in the winter. Mules are slow to begin with. A tired one may as well walk backwards."

Soapy laughed and slapped Joe on the knee again. "You're right, Joe. If I ride a mule, we're lost." He laughed harder. "But everything that *looks* like a mule, *isn't*. How about *those* apples?"

Joe put the Stetson back on his head and tugged it down

tight. He was beginning to worry that his new-found friend might have soap in his head instead of brains.

It did not take long for Joe to learn that Soapy loved to talk. He would talk about anything, as long as he thought Joe might be listening. Between the never-ending slamming of the stamp mill and Soapy's never-ending stories, Joe thought he might go deaf himself.

"Say, Soapy," Joe said, finally finding a place in one of his stories where he could interrupt without seeming overly rude. "I'm kind of hungry. I haven't had anything to eat except water for a day and a half. Is there anywhere in the camp I can buy something to eat? I'll settle for anything— eggs, bacon, pancakes."

"No need to throw away your money, Joe. I've got all the food we need. Those varmints who sold your horse to the mine bosses, sold 'em sixteen head of prime Colorado cattle, as well. I got to the butcher's early, and was able to trade a little gold powder for a whole leg of beef. We've got enough to last us several days, if we can keep the rats off it."

Wham!

The stamp mill shattered the air with another rock-crushing blow.

"Those were Missus Summerlin's cattle, Soapy. *Those* rats sold *our* stock. I want to catch them more than ever."

Wham!

"Tell you what, Joe. Let's get out of here for a while." Soapy stood up and began throwing supplies in a burlap bag. He added a large pot, two gold pans, and a slab of beef wrapped in oiled paper. He looked around for a minute and added a small burlap bag of potatoes and a bag of beans.

"Let's go mining," Soapy said when he had the bag filled up. He picked up a short shovel and threw it on his shoulder.

"Mining?" Joe asked. "I thought we were going to eat."

"We *are* going to eat. There's a place just over the ridge, on a stream that carries a little gold fleck every now and then. I spend most of my daylight hours there, panning through the gravel. The ridge cuts off the sound of the stamper, and I find enough gold to keep me in taters and beans. The stream doesn't have any big nuggets—not enough gold in it for most of these men. They can make more money working for the mine bosses, but it suits me because it's quieter. You know how to pan for gold?"

"Nope."

Soapy grinned. "Good. I'll teach you. Then you can pan while I cook. Of course, we both need to be on the lookout for Snake In the Grass." He winked at Joe and opened the crate he had been sitting on earlier. He took out several items that Joe could not see.

It took Joe and Soapy half an hour to reach Soapy's stream.

Soapy started a fire, put a pot of water in the middle of it, and dumped in the beef from the oiled paper. He added about two handfuls of red kidney beans from the bean bag.

"I'm not much of a cook," Soapy said. "But the meat and beans will fill us up, Joe. It'll give us the energy we need for tonight."

Soapy handed Joe one of the pans and showed him how to wash for gold.

"Dig up some gravel from the stream bed, and toss it on the bank. Grab a handful and put it in the pan. Then you wash the pan in the creek, moving it back and forth, like this." Soapy showed Joe his method.

"Gold is heavy, and will sink to the bottom of the pan. Just let the lighter gravel and sand wash out. Then look close at the screen in the bottom. You'll know if you get any gold. It'll stick out like a sore thumb. Here. You try it."

Joe took the pan and began washing the gravel. It took him several tries before Soapy considered him good enough to go it alone.

"Did you see him?" Soapy asked in a hushed voice. "Don't gawk! Look out of the corner of your eyes. He's about fifty feet away, behind that clump of wire-grass bushes off to your right."

Joe strained his eyes, keeping his head pointed toward the stream, but he could not detect anyone else within a hundred paces of them.

"Can't *see* him, Soapy."

"Just keep panning, Joe. He's good. Like I told you, that's why we call him Snake In the Grass. Try to ignore him. If he suspects we know he's there, he'll run like a scared rabbit."

Soapy took the other pan and moved several paces downstream. He tossed several shovels of gravel on the stream bank and handed the shovel back to Joe. Soapy then began panning in earnest.

"You haven't asked me how I got to be named Soapy, yet," he said.

"No. I haven't." Joe washed out a pan of gravel, still searching in vain out of the corners of his eyes for the man who was spying on them.

"It's sort of a backwards name," Soapy said.

"Backwards? How so?"

"Because I don't hardly ever take a bath!" he said, laughing loudly. "And when I do, I *never* use soap!" Soapy stared hard at Joe. "Pssst!"

Joe glanced up, then turned his head abruptly away. "Yeah?" he whispered.

"He's moved closer, Joe. I'm gonna keep telling you my story—and I'm gonna speak real loud, so's he can hear us. You talk loud, too."

Joe stopped panning and stared at Soapy. He nodded. "Why don't you ever use soap?" he asked, almost shouting.

"Pee-you!" Soapy replied. "Makes a man smell like perfume! I prefer to smell just like I am." In a lower voice, he added, "That's good, Joe. Keep it up."

"Then why do they call you Soapy?"

"Because soap saved my life."

"It did?" Joe quit panning and stared at the man again. "How?"

"Before I tell you," Soapy said loudly, "I think we need to hide these gold flakes I found. How about in the potato sack, Joe?"

"Sounds good to me, Soapy. No one would think to look in a potato sack for gold."

Soapy pulled out the burlap bag with the potatoes in it, and emptied about half of them onto the ground. Then he added several other items to the bag. Joe could swear he saw smoke coming from the bag, but he pretended not to notice. Soapy took the bag and carried it about twenty paces away, covering it up with several rocks.

"No one will see it now, Joe." He returned to the stream bed and continued with his story.

"One winter, about six years ago, me and another old-timer went prospecting up in Wyoming territory. We reached the spot we wanted in the summer, and had plenty enough time to build a small cabin and lay in firewood for the winter. Come September, we decided he would go down to the nearest big camp and lay in supplies. He was going to get flour, and cornmeal, and taters and such. Food. We hadn't stocked any food, because we thought we had plenty of time. No sooner does he get gone, than a huge, early-winter storm comes through, laying down about three feet of snow, and I was stuck inside the cabin." Soapy continued to pan while he talked.

Joe turned slightly, so he could keep an eye on the potato sack. He was curious to catch sight of this man Soapy called the Snake In the Grass.

"All I had to eat was a half-pound of cornmeal," Soapy went on. "And it ran out after two days. The snow lasted three weeks. And there was no way my partner could get through to me, neither. I had plenty of water, of course, from the snow. But I didn't have any vittles."

"What did you eat?" Joe asked. "How did you live that long without any food?"

"I ate soap."

"What?" Joe sat back on the bank, setting his pan beside him. "You're joking. You must be pulling my leg." He used this opportunity to scan the area where Soapy had planted the potato sack. Then he saw him.

No wonder the man was difficult to see—not only was he thin as a tree trunk, he wore old, dirty, homemade canvas slacks and a shirt that were the exact color of the rocks and boulders he crept among. If Joe had not known to be looking for the man, he'd have never seen him.

In an instant, the man had grabbed the potato sack and was gone.

"You see him?" Soapy asked.

Joe nodded. "What now?"

"Nothin'. We just wait."

"Wouldn't it be better to go after him, Soapy?"

"Nope. No need. All he's got is a sack of taters and a blasting cap. It's lit and set to go off in less than a minute."

Now Joe remembered. He *had* seen smoke.

"Won't he notice the smoke from the fuse?"

"Sure he will. But most of the time, Joe, a thief won't use his common sense. He'll be so excited about getting something for nothing, he won't recognize the fuse for what it really is until it's too late."

Joe shook his head and grinned. "Yeah. You're probably right. But go on—that part about you eating soap—you were kidding. Right?"

"Nope. The man I partnered with was a washing fool. He loved to take baths. I do believe that's what finally killed him, too. He caught cold after one of his baths."

"Nothing wrong with a bath," Joe said, eyeing Soapy with new respect. "But finish the story. I'm eager to hear how it ends."

"That washing fool had stockpiled a whole cask of bear grease and a tin of lye to make soap out of. He had enough soap makings for ten years, if you ask me, but he claimed it would barely get him through the winter." Soapy paused to wash out a pan of gravel.

"Anyway, my partner had taken the grease and made up fifty little cakes out of it. He had them all lined up along the floor of the cabin, just waiting for him to add the lye." Soapy began laughing so hard he spilled all the gravel out of his pan.

"I was glad he had left before he finished, to go after supplies, too. Because, I got so hungry, I'd have eaten that bear grease even if it *did* have lye in it. Whee-hoo!" Soapy laughed so hard he had to hold on to his pan with both hands.

"You should have seen how mad that feller was when he finally got through to me and found out I had eaten all his soap makings. He went all winter without a single soaped-up bath. He smelled just fine to me. Ha! And I've been called Soapy ever since."

Joe shook his head and glanced up at Soapy. "How much longer before that blasting cap—"

Ka-whump!

"Got him!" Soapy yelled. "Heh-heh-heh. That rascal will have his fingers singed so bad he won't be able to steal nothin' for six months!"

As soon as he stopped laughing, Soapy poured out some beef and beans onto two tin plates, handing one to Joe. Joe was so hungry he felt *he* could eat bear grease. He picked up a piece of beef and stuck it in his mouth, chewing as fast as he could. Joe tried his best to keep from making a face. The beef was the worst he had ever eaten. He glanced at the setting sun as he chewed, wishing Chili were here to do the cooking. Chili's meals were always a little spicy, but they were also always very tasty. Joe ate as fast as he could.

"What's your rush?" Soapy asked, looking up into the sky toward the afternoon sun. "We ain't in no hurry, Joe. Snake In the Grass is gone, and the sun won't set for hours. We got nothin' to do but eat and pan for gold. Life couldn't get much better than this, could it?"

Joe finished gulping down his meal and did not ask for seconds. He could not bring himself to tell Soapy that he wanted the afternoon *and* the meal over just as fast as possible.

Chapter Nine

Aﬁter they finished eating, Soapy and Joe went back to panning for gold. Joe became more and more bored with every panful.

Joe finally tossed his pan down in disgust. He did not have any luck panning for gold.

"Sorry, Soapy," he said. "I'm just not cut out to be a miner." He wiped the sweat from his brow. At least the noise from the stamp mill was muffled by the hill.

"Don't worry, Joe. I found enough for both of us. Seven flakes. It's common, the first time out, to come up empty-handed. These flakes I found will buy us all the taters we need. Hey—you ready for some more beef and beans?"

"Uh . . . nope." Joe realized he had been spoiled by Chili's cooking.

A sudden, troubling thought occurred to Joe. "What if someone steals all your powder and dynamite while we're out here panning, Soapy? We just walked off and left all your explosives in the back of your tent. What if someone strolls in and takes them?"

"They won't."

"Why not? What's to stop them?"

Soapy held up his hand with the missing three fingers. "This," he said. "Like I told you earlier, I keep the miners scared. I tell 'em how lots of greenhorn powder men I've known got blowed to Kingdom Come. I tell 'em it can happen from just moving a single crate of dynamite from one spot to another."

Joe shivered. He had recently been sitting on just such a case of dynamite.

"You were lying to them, weren't you, Soapy? A crate of dynamite can't just blow up, can it? Didn't you tell me that we were safe, sitting on the dynamite in your tent?"

"I might have told you a little white lie, Joe—to make you feel more comfortable. Happens all the time, actually." Soapy chewed contentedly on a large wad of beef, pulling it out of his mouth now and then to see if it was ready to swallow.

"One bad move, Joe," he went on, "and, blooie! More than fingers gets blowed off, too. I've seen arms, legs, necks—"

"Whoa!" Joe called out. "I get the picture." He was not so sure he wanted to return to Soapy's tent after hearing about how temperamental dynamite could be.

"What about our plan, Soapy? Have you given any thought to what we're going to do to rescue Davey?"

"Plan? What plan, Joe?"

"Remember? You said we were going to plan our moves for tonight while we were panning for gold."

"Oh. That plan. I got a little sidetracked by old Snake In the Grass. But don't worry. I'll come up with something." He paused, deep in thought, for several moments.

"I got it, Joe."

"Well, come on. Aren't you going to tell me?"

"Sure I am. The plan is . . . we're gonna light a bunch of dynamite and blow the roof off. That's our plan."

Joe took off his Stetson, scooped up some water in it, and placed it back on his head, water and all. It was hot and he needed to cool off. Plus, he could not believe that Soapy had no more of a plan than "blow the roof off," and he felt that the cool water would relieve his tension.

"Is that all?" he asked Soapy. "Just blow the roof off? What roof?"

"Blow the roof off is just a manner of speaking, Joe. We powder men use it all the time. It doesn't mean we're going to actually blow a real roof off. It means we're going to blow things up. It can be anything." He stopped and took a long swig of the beans and beef broth, wiping his mouth with his shirt sleeve.

"Say, Joe, did I ever tell you about the time I lived in a mine shaft?" Without looking at Joe, Soapy picked up his pan and began sifting for gold again.

"No, Soapy. But let's get back to our plan again."

"It was about four years ago," Soapy said, ignoring Joe's request. "I didn't have a tent then, much less the pegs to tie it down, so I just pitched camp deep inside an abandoned silver mine shaft."

"That's real interesting, Soapy. But what's that got to do with our plan?"

"The only problem about living deep inside a mine shaft is that you never know whether it's day or night, morning or afternoon. It's always dark 'cause you've got no windows. You just go to sleep when you're tired, and hope it's light outside when you wake up."

"Yeah, Soapy. But what—"

"One time I woke up, thinking it might be morning, and I was so tired I walked off in the wrong direction. Instead of heading *out* of the shaft, I went in *deeper*. This was one of those big shafts, too. Some outfit out of San Francisco owned it, and those rascals burrowed holes all over that mountain, as if they were sure-enough gophers. Guess they found a silver vein that zigged and zagged, and they followed it every turn it made. When I finally realized I wasn't on my way out, it was too late. There I was, slap in the middle of a mountain criss-crossed with nearly a hundred or more tunnels. Gopher Town, I called it." Soapy dumped the gravel out of his pan and filled it again.

"Took me nearly four days to get out, Joe. And I never did find the shaft I started out camping in. I took off out of that place, leaving all my gear and everything, and I never went back. That broke me of living in mine shafts, too. I've been in tents or shacks ever since. No, sir! You won't catch old Soapy doing either one of two things: I don't take baths, and I don't live in mine shafts."

Nor make plans, Joe thought. *What a mess I have got myself into. I've got a partner with soap for brains, who'll probably blow us both to Kingdom Come.*

"Joe! Joe! Wake up!"

"Huh? What?" Joe turned on his bedroll and opened his eyes. It was beginning to turn cool, yet he was sweating. He realized why—he had been dreaming about Tommy. Just before dark, Joe and Soapy had returned to the tent to try and get a few hours' sleep, and he was having a nightmare. He closed his eyes to collect his thoughts and try to calm down. He was under a lot of stress to find the young boy, and was making very little headway. He knew the longer it took him to locate Tommy, the worse the chance of finding him alive would be. Joe also knew that if he had to ride back to the Summerlin ranch alone, Emma would never forgive him.

All the stress he was under caused him to have bad dreams. He opened his eyes again and looked up to see Soapy staring at him four inches away.

"Did we sleep long, Soapy?" Joe glanced past the grizzled face to the front of the tent. He could see that it was dark outside.

"About two hours," Soapy said. "You were plenty tired, I reckon." Soapy went to his own bedroll, which he began rolling in a tight bundle. When finished, he tied a rope around it several times.

Joe stretched, unwilling to rise. "We still don't have a plan, Soapy," he said. "I wish we had a plan."

Soapy grunted and cocked his head to one side, as if unsure he heard Joe correctly.

"Why, we do have a plan, Joe." He thumped his forehead with his index finger.

"It's all up here, partner. I've got the plan mapped out from start to finish, from packing our gear to riding our way out of here."

"You've got it all in your head, huh?" Joe rolled over, got up, and slowly began working on his own bedroll. He was not too sure he could depend on Soapy's detailed plan.

"What's first, then, Soapy? What do we do now?"

"We pack up. That's what I just finished telling you, Joe. We pack our gear."

Who-hoot!

The sudden blare of a horn cut through the air, causing Joe to jump. All other sounds in the camp were silenced after the horn.

"What the tarnation was that?" Joe asked, embarrassed for Soapy to see how jumpy he was.

"The warning horn. We've got ten minutes, then another horn will sound. One minute after that one, the dynamite is set off in the tunnel. The horns warn everybody to clear out." Soapy tossed his bedroll to the front of the tent.

"Come on, Joe. We're running out of time. I've got all the planning done, but if we don't get a move on, it won't do us any good. We've got to pack up."

Working as Soapy directed, Joe helped him load up the supplies for their getaway. They placed all of the items at the front of the tent where Soapy had put his bedroll. They collected one box of black powder, two canvas bags of dynamite, two bags of blasting caps, a bag of loose lead shot, a bag of fuses and wadding materials, matches, a box of cheap cigars, two large bags of foodstuffs, and an even larger bag of mining tools. In the mining-tool bag was a shovel, a pick, two sifting pans, and empty sacks for gold dust and nuggets.

"Why cigars?" Joe asked. "I haven't seen you smoke one since I've been here."

"I don't smoke much," Soapy said. "Those are my lighters."

"Lighters?"

"Yep. For lighting fuses. You light the cigar with a match, then wait until you're ready to light the fuse. A cigar lasts longer than a match and is harder to see in the night by prying eyes than a match striking up in the dark. If it's windy, your match will blow out just when you need it most, too. A man can light a bunch of fuses with one cigar, but only one or two with a good match." Soapy grinned maliciously. "And when push comes to shove, Joe, I plan on lighting a *bundle* of fuses."

Joe nodded. He was becoming an expert in dynamiting, a career he had never been very interested in, since most powder men he had known were missing more fingers than Soapy.

The gear made an impressive pile in the front of the tent.

"Wish we could take more," Soapy said. "But I don't see how we'd manage."

"I don't see how we can carry all *that*," Joe said, pointing to the stack of supplies.

Soapy cocked his head at Joe again. "Didn't you tell me your horse was strong, Joe? Strong enough to carry you and gear at the same time."

"Well, yes. But we'll be so slowed down by the weight of all that stuff, we'll be as easy to catch as a three-legged deer."

"No such way," Soapy snapped back. He was hurt that Joe did not seem to trust his ability to plan well. He held up one of the bags of dynamite.

"This bag has caps already attached to the dynamite," Soapy said. "And a three-legged deer ain't got *these!*"

Who-hoot!

The horn sounded for the second time, once again causing Joe to jump.

Soapy began counting out loud, from sixty down to zero.

Just as he reached zero, the explosion in the mine tunnel went off, shaking the very ground beneath their feet.

All other sounds in the camp were silenced for several moments after the blast.

Soapy quickly divided the gear at the front of the tent in two halves. Joe noticed there was dynamite in each pile.

Soapy reached in one of the food bags and pulled out two potatoes, handing one to Joe.

"For your horse," Soapy said. "They don't feed 'em too good down at the mine, so he'll need it. Once we create our little diversion, we'll bring our steeds back here, load up the supplies, then move out."

Soapy walked to the front of the tent and pointed to the pile of materials on the right.

"That one will be yours, Joe. The bags all have canvas or rope straps, but tie 'em on your horse with an extra rope. Understand? We can't be too careful. We can't afford to lose any of these supplies."

Joe nodded, staring intently at the pile of goods Soapy wanted him to tie on to Davey's back.

"There's one of the bags of dynamite in my stack," Joe said. "Didn't you tell me the dynamite was dangerous to carry? Are you sure I should put it on my horse? It'll be right behind my back."

"Sure, it's dangerous," Soapy said. "But as long as you got all the dynamite, and I'm carrying the caps, it'll be difficult to make it blow up on us."

"How about the bag you've got?" Joe asked. "The one with dynamite *and* caps, already assembled."

"Oh, that one's only trouble for us if a stray bullet happens to hit it," Soapy said. "Yep. If we're riding side-by-side, and a bullet hits *that* bag, we won't give a hill of beans whether we find those kidnappers or not, Joe. We'll be blasted up beyond the clouds!"

Chapter Ten

J oe was amazed at how organized and sure of himself Soapy turned out to be. The grizzled prospector proceeded as if he really did have a plan, though Joe was still skeptical about that.

Soapy carefully stuck three of his pre-made dynamite charges in his trousers' pockets. "Come on, Joe. It's time," he said, leading the way out of the tent.

Each of the explosive charges Soapy had put together consisted of two sticks of dynamite, a blasting cap, and a ten-minute fuse.

Joe followed Soapy down the hill, toward the stamp mill. It was dark, and Joe was glad to have Soapy leading the way through the maze of tents, sheds, and other obstacles. The most difficult of the obstacles to see were the open garbage pits, containing grease, bones, and rotting vegetables, and the human waste pits, which were nothing more than holes dug in the ground several feet deep, with a thin layer of dirt thrown over them after each use. After threading their way past several of these different pits, Joe was extremely glad to have Soapy as his guide.

"Where is everyone?" Joe asked, when they were about halfway down the hill. "It's deserted." They had not yet passed a single person on their trek.

Soapy stopped and pointed across the valley. "See where it's lit up over yonder?"

"Yep. What is it? A meeting of some sort."

"Not really. It's not a town, because it's just like all these structures—tents and ramshackle wood buildings. But it's the closest thing to a town hereabouts. It's a bunch of dance halls, saloons, and gambling shacks. Soon as the horn blares and the dynamite is set off in the tunnel, every miner in Lost Gulch with a fleck of gold in his pocket heads for that area." Soapy laughed, then began walking down the hill again, Joe close behind so he would not step into any unseen holes.

"There's more fools," Soapy went on, "ready to part with their money around here, than there are fools in the whole rest of the state put together. Heh-heh! I was one of 'em, too. That's the *sad* part. Heh-heh!"

As they neared the bottom of the valley, Soapy stopped to light up a cigar. Joe was worried that Soapy was using the cigar to pause and reflect. He was worried that Soapy did not have an actual plan after all.

Soapy began walking again, without so much as a word, and within minutes they reached the stamp mill. They stood silently for a few seconds. All seemed to be still. Joe continued to be amazed at how deserted the place seemed to be, but he could hear music and shouting coming from the lit-up area Soapy had told him about.

The stamp mill machinery was housed in a building behind a six-foot-tall fence. Where the railroad tracks from the mine went into the mill was a large double gate, now closed and locked fast. They walked around the fenced compound, until they almost reached the other side, and Soapy stopped. He pointed to another gate in the fence.

"That's where the men go in," he whispered to Joe. "It's closed and locked, too, but it's the only gate they guard. Come on. Our work is on the other end."

Soapy led Joe back to the gate over the tracks and stopped again.

"I guess we won't be blowing up the stamp mill, then," Joe said softly. "We can't get inside."

"You're right," Soapy said. "*We* can't go inside, but *this* can." He held up one of his dynamite charges. "Make your hands into a step for me, Joe, then boost me up. It's time to act."

Joe clasped his hands together and leaned against the wooden gate of the fence for support. Soapy stuck one foot in Joe's hands, and boosted himself upwards, using Joe's shoulder as a handhold. Several hot ashes from Soapy's still-lit cigar fell on Joe's face, but he did not move or make a sound.

Soapy's shoulders were now at the top of the fence. He lit the fuse to the dynamite and threw it as hard as he could.

"Bull's-eye!" Soapy yelled when he saw the dynamite land. Joe was worried the guards might have heard him.

"Come on down, Soapy. Let's go."

The powder man hopped to the ground and trotted off, Joe once more close behind.

"Where did it land?" Joe asked. "Will it do any damage? I don't see how, from that distance. The building had to be thirty paces from the fence."

"I wasn't aiming for the building," Soapy said. "I aimed for the boiler, which is kept outside for safety reasons. The dynamite rolled right up under it, too."

"What good will that do us?" Joe asked.

"It'll put the mine bosses out of business for a while, Joe. It won't blow up the whole works, but they'll have a big hole in the boiler tank. Without that, they won't have steam. Without steam, they won't be able to power the stamper and crush the rock. It'll be several weeks before they can repair it, because the only fellers who do that kind of work are working on a mine in Nevada. Heh-heh!"

In less than a minute, Soapy stopped Joe at a point on the railroad tracks. "We're halfway between the tunnel and the stamp mill. This will give 'em something else to worry about, and they won't be able to use any animals on it until they get it repaired."

Soapy pulled out another dynamite package and lit the fuse with the cigar. He placed the charge gently beside one of the tracks, and motioned for Joe to follow him.

"Come on," he said. "We have to move faster now. The first charge will blow in about eight minutes, then this one will go off. I used ten-minute fuses on each of them. We don't have a lot of time left."

"How are you so sure the fuses will be on time?" Joe asked. "Didn't you tell me some of the fuses you came across were one-minute instead of ten-minute?"

"I test all my fuses nowadays," Soapy said, as he continued to walk. He held up his hand with the missing fingers. "I don't want this to happen again. Of course, those are actually all *nine-minute* fuses now, because I burned a whole minute off of each one, testing 'em! Heh-heh! Let's hurry, Joe!"

When they arrived at the corral, Joe realized that Soapy had been right again. There were no guards stationed here.

They opened the gate and Joe immediately saw why no guards were needed. Normally, when a stock gate was opened, it was difficult to herd the animals back, to keep them from trying to escape. This was a different matter. These animals had been so mistreated, and were so malnourished, that none of them made the slightest effort to get out. Not even Davey, and that fact worried Joe more than anything. He hoped desperately that the horse's spirit had not been broken.

He whistled, but there was no response. "Davey!" he called out as loud as he dared. "Come on, fella. It's me. Davey! Are you okay? Come on!"

There was no response. Davey did not come bounding out of the small, subdued herd of unfortunate animals at the other end of the corral. Nor did he answer Joe with a proud neigh. Joe's heart sunk. If Davey was not here, or if he was dead, Joe was not sure what he would do next. He was not even sure it would be worth it to continue on.

"What're you doing to the horses, Joe?" Soapy asked, a worried expression on his face. "You've got 'em all upset."

"How? What do you mean?"

"See over there? By the far fence? Some rascal horse is kicking and thumping the fence with his head, as if he's trying to tear the whole place down."

Joe did not ask any more questions. He ran to the far fence.

"Davey! No wonder you didn't come to me."

Joe had never seen Davey under such constraints. The poor animal was not only tied to the fence by his reins, he had a rope tied off around his snout to keep him from biting, and was hobbled with a rope tied around his rear legs. Davey kicked out with joy when he saw Joe.

Joe gave Davey a hug, then began untying the ropes. He wept as he saw the welts and bruises on Davey's back and haunches made by the mine bosses' bull whip.

When Davey calmed down, Joe cut up the potato Soapy had given him, and he fed it to the half-starved horse, piece by piece. Joe grabbed Davey's bridle and led him toward the gate. Soapy began herding the other animals ahead of him, but Joe could not yet tell which one was Soapy's steed.

"Are you going to set off the third charge here?" Joe asked.

"Nope. It's for a special place. My plan is to drive all of these poor animals out of the corral, and hope that a few of them make it to permanent freedom in the hills. That's as much as we can do for 'em, Joe."

"Where's your horse?" Joe asked. As he gazed around at the animals left in the pen, he did not see any other horses. They all looked like mules.

"Come on," Soapy said. "The saddles are in the shed outside. I've got my ride right here. Let's hurry. We've only got about five minutes left."

Joe gasped. Soapy was leading a mule by the bridle.

"Soapy?" Joe said as loud as he dared. "That's a mule! You can't ride out of here on a mule. We'll be done for."

Soapy and the animal he was leading came to a sudden stop.

"Look closer, Joe. It's dark, and your eyes ain't working real good. This ain't a mule, she's a Shetland pony!"

Joe approached the animal and peered closely, surprised to find out Soapy was telling the truth.

The Shetland pony suddenly reached out and nipped Joe on the arm.

"Ouch! Dang, Soapy. She bit me. If she *isn't* a Shetland pony, she sure bites like one."

"This is Devil, Joe. Aptly named, as you can tell. She's easily the meanest little Shetland pony I ever did own. She kind of reminds me of myself, I reckon. But she's also the strongest and most reliable ride I ever did own, too. She can carry me and a hundred pounds of gear all day long, without a rest. Of course, she'll bite me about seventeen times in a day, too, complaining to me about how hard I'm working her. She's small, mean, and as big-hearted as they come."

Soapy swatted off several flies that had gathered on Devil's back where the leather lash had cut through her skin, leaving splotches of dried-up blood.

"Dad-gummed mine bosses," Soapy said. "No animal deserves this kind of treatment, Joe." He rubbed Devil's neck affectionately as he fed her the potato.

"It's all my fault, too. I lost Devil in a poker game two weeks ago to another miner. He had a full house to my three queens. I still don't see how I lost. Before I could get up enough money to buy her back, the rascal sold her to the mine bosses, and they wouldn't let me buy her."

Devil nipped Soapy on the arm, as if she could actually understand what he was saying.

"I don't have any more taters," Soapy said to the pony. "Come on, girl. Soon as we get clear of this place, I'll feed you a whole sack of 'em. I promise." He turned to Joe.

"Let's get on with it. We need to be saddled up and on our way to the tent, where we can load our gear. Pronto!"

Joe was thankful to find his saddle among all the livery items thrown in piles in the shed. As soon as he and Soapy had the horse and pony saddled up, they mounted and rode out.

"We're going to go *around* the tents this time," Soapy said. "We can't take the chance of Devil or Davey stepping in a garbage hole and breaking a leg. Let's ride!"

They reached the top of the hill and pulled up to Soapy's tent. Both men went to work, tying on the gear as fast as they could. Joe did not think they could load all of it, but they were finished in just a few minutes. He was also worried that the first blast would go off before they had a chance to leave, and some stray lookout would tell the mine bosses which way they went.

Joe mounted Davey, careful not to put too much pressure anywhere there was a welt from the whip. "I'm ready, Soapy," he said.

"One last detail, Joe." Soapy pulled the still-lit cigar out of his mouth and ran back in the tent. In just a few seconds, he came running out, mounted Devil, and they rode off.

"That was one last little present for the mine bosses, Joe," Soapy said after they had cleared the camp. "This one will leave a big hole in the ground for them to wonder about. Some of them will think we got blown up with it, and argue against following us. It'll slow 'em down a little, if nothing else."

Joe saw that Soapy had been right about Devil. The pony was small, but she kept up with Davey every step of the way.

Joe and Soapy kept both animals to a medium trot. They realized their steeds were tired and worn out from working the ore carts, and they did not want to over-exert them.

Ka-blam!

Joe glanced back and saw the red glow at the stamp mill, where the first charge had been lit. Soapy had planned well. They were far enough away to have a good lead on any posse that might try to follow them.

Ka-bloom!

The second charge at the railroad tracks went off sooner than Joe expected, but at least it did detonate.

"Gee-up, Davey!" he shouted.

"High-tail it outta here, Devil!" Soapy yelled.

Davey and Devil, free at last, ran with all their hearts.

Chapter Eleven

Joe and Soapy would ride for close to an hour, then dismount and walk beside Davey and Devil. This way they continued to make forward progress without tiring their mounts.

Joe was determined to put as much distance between them and Lost Gulch as he could. He was not anxious for a posse to come up behind them, shooting away. Especially since Soapy still had a full bag of blasting caps in a bag packed on Devil.

They were on the same trail Joe had started out on earlier, heading north, for most of the night. Soapy finally recommended they make camp and let the horses rest.

"It's as if we're making them work a double shift," Soapy said. "The poor animals have already worked a full day, and now we're pushing them all night."

Joe agreed and they set up camp in a sheltered area

87

above the trail. This way, if a posse was on their trail, it might pass by, never seeing them.

Soapy and Joe unpacked and fed Davey and Devil before they did anything else. Devil nipped Soapy twice and Joe once, and Joe learned to stay out of her range. Soapy did not seem to mind the bites. In fact, he actually seemed to enjoy the attention from Devil, even though it hurt.

Each animal was fed a potato and a handful of grain, then they were allowed to roam free, eating grass.

"You're not worried that Davey will run off?" Soapy asked.

"Nope. How about Devil? I've never known a Shetland pony to hang around if she had half a chance to move on."

"No way. Me and Devil are partners, and she knows it. She won't leave me unless it's in my own best interest."

After a quick meal of boiled potatoes and beef, Soapy covered the fire with dirt and the two men fell fast asleep.

As soon as the sun rose, they were up, saddled, and moving out. They did not even take time to make coffee. The weather had turned cold overnight, and Joe and Soapy both wanted to move so they would warm up naturally before they stopped to rest again.

"I believe Idaho Springs is just ahead," Soapy said. "We should be there before nightfall. It's not supposed to be much of a town, but we can replenish our food and rest up a while there."

"I just hope they have some news about the horse rustlers," Joe said. "Why is a town in Colorado named *Idaho* Springs, anyway?"

"Got me," Soapy replied. "Probably some miner from Idaho got homesick and figured it was as good a name as any. Who knows?"

Ka-pow!

A bullet ricocheted off the cliff wall above them, startling both men and steeds.

The sound of the rifle shot closely followed.

Joe glanced back, then urged Davey forward. "A posse!" he yelled. "Three to four hundred paces, judging by the time it took us to hear the rifle. Come on!"

Joe led the way up the ravine to the shelter of the many large rocks above. He wanted to be on higher ground while he reconnoitered the group that was behind them. He felt they could run from the posse as well from above the trail, as from below.

When they reached the top and dismounted, Joe gazed intently back down the trail, trying to sight the men who had shot at them. Soapy pulled a telescope from his backpack and handed it to Joe.

"Your eyes are younger than mine," he said. "You peek through the lens. I won it in a poker game, just before I lost Devil. Only thing I ever won that was worth more than ten cents, too."

Joe found the posse in the telescope and counted five men on horseback, one on the ground. The man on the ground had a rifle propped on top of a boulder, aimed straight at them.

"Get your head down!" Joe yelled, and both men ducked. "They've got a sharpshooter. It looks like he's carrying a

Springfield rifle. If he gets a good bead on us, we're goners."

Ka-pow!

Another bullet ricocheted off a nearby rock.

Joe looked around where they had stopped and realized
that there would be no way to outrun the posse from up
here. Boulders and rocks of all sizes littered the landscape,
piled high atop one another. They looked as if they would
come crashing down at any time, and there was no way he
and Soapy could safely and quickly pass through them.

"This will be a good place to hold a gun battle," Joe
said. "But that's about all. The only trail out of here is the
one we were just on."

"This is as good a place as any, then," Soapy said.

"I think we should head back down and try to outrun
them," Joe said.

"If those thugs are from the mine," Soapy said, "they'll
be the worst sort of ruffians the mine bosses could round
up. They won't have any 'dead or alive' orders from the
mine bosses, either. Their orders will be 'dead or deader.'
We can't outrun them with tired mounts, Joe. Plus, we're
loaded down heavier than they are. How many are there?"

"Six."

"We can't outshoot 'em then, either. We've only got one
choice, Joe."

"One choice? What's that? I'm not going to give up,
Soapy."

"Give up? Never! I'm a powder man, Joe. No self-
respecting powder man *ever* gives up. You take Davey and

Devil back down to the trail. Move on down about thirty paces and wait for me there. I've got a plan, Joe."

Soapy went to the pack on Devil's back and began unloading, pulling out dynamite, caps, and a cigar.

"Go on, Joe. I'll be down lickety-split."

Joe reluctantly led both animals back down the ravine and walked northward forty paces. He wanted the extra ten paces just in case that Springfield rifle caught one of the blasting caps Soapy was carrying.

Ka-pow!

The bullet bounced off a rock off to Soapy's left. The sharpshooter was trying to pick him off, but Soapy scrambled to and fro among the large boulders, rarely making a suitable target for the shooter.

Ka-pow!

Joe was afraid to watch. The shooter might get Soapy's range any time and hit a cap with a lucky shot. Seconds later Soapy came scampering down the hill.

He stopped in the middle of the trail and gently set his cigar down, then ran up to Devil and mounted.

"Let's go, Joe!" he yelled. "We'll ride off about a hundred paces, stop, and take positions on the top of the ravine again."

"Don't you think we should just keep going?" Joe asked. "A hundred paces is like a turkey shoot for a man with a Springfield rifle."

"Nope. We go a hundred paces, then watch the cigar. Any further and we won't be able to see it."

"The cigar? Are you crazy?"

"Nope. Come on, and I'll explain once we hunker down."

Cigar? Joe thought as they rode up the trail. *We're going to stop and watch a cigar? Soapy has lost his mind!*

By the time Joe and Soapy had gone a hundred paces, the trail took a sharp turn to the right, so Joe figured it might not be such a poor location to fight from after all. Soapy agreed.

"The sharpshooter won't be able to see us until they reach the cigar," he said. "That's perfect. We'll be out of his range until then."

They dismounted and led Davey and Devil to the top of the ravine once again. This section was covered by as many stones and boulders as the other had been, Joe noticed. They tied the animals to some shrubs, to keep them from being spooked when the shooting started.

Joe and Soapy took up positions behind one of the smaller boulders, so they could look over the top, rather than around the sides.

"Okay, Soapy," Joe said, as he knelt behind the rock. "Tell me about the cigar. What's so important about it?" He rested his Colt on top to steady his aim, though he realized the revolver was no match for a Springfield rifle.

Soapy laughed. "It's all got to do with human nature, Joe. We're going to take advantage of human nature. That's what."

"Go on."

"When those six bounty hunters reach that part of the trail where the cigar is sitting, sending up a thin plume of

smoke to catch their attention, they're not going to be able
to resist it. They'll stop, and one of 'em will climb off his
horse to investigate."

"Yeah? I can see that. But so what? All they'll find is
an old cigar."

"Well, Joe. No hardscrabble miner will be able to resist
what he thinks is a free cigar. Especially one already lit
and slobbered over. He won't be able to pass it up."

Joe could not see how a man would pick up and smoke
another man's cigar.

"So what?" he said. "Some miner gets a free cigar. What
does that do for us?"

"It gives us time, Joe. That'll be all the time we need,
right then and there. And if I've still got it in me, we'll be
home free and out of here, with no one on our tails."

"I'm still puzzled, Soapy. If you've still got *what* in you?
And I don't see how we're going to be home free. Looks
to me more like we've both stepped off into one of those
garbage pits back in Lost Gulch, and we're up to our necks
in stinking filth."

"Nope. What I'm talking about, Joe, is whether or not
I've still got the powder knack. A powder man's gotta have
the knack. He's gotta know where to set his charge, how
much of a charge to set, and when to blow her. I've got to
see if I've still got that knack, Joe. Setting off a few little
charges like we did back at Lost Gulch doesn't prove anything. *This* will prove everything!"

"I hope you've still got the knack, too, Soapy, because
if you don't, this time we're goners for certain."

"I'd rather be a goner, Joe, than lose the knack. A powder man is as worthless as a played-out mine if he loses the knack."

"Shh!" Joe whispered. "There they are."

The six men of the posse had stopped, just as Soapy had predicted, right on top of the cigar.

Joe put the telescope to his eye and watched.

The lead man jumped off his horse and carefully examined the still-lit cigar as it lay on the ground. More than half of it was left. He picked it up, eyed it all around, then stuck it in his mouth and chomped down on it.

"It's nearly time, Joe," Soapy said. "You go get the horses and be ready to move. I'll wave my arms to keep their attention and to keep them in one spot."

"I think we should both go and run for it, Soapy." Joe still peered through the telescope. He watched as the man with the Springfield dismounted and propped the rifle on top of another boulder.

Soapy rose up, waving his arms. "You just get the horses, Joe. Trust me on this."

Ka-thud!

The bullet kicked up dust as it hit solid dirt, not more than three paces from Soapy.

Joe scrambled away, after Davey and Devil. He hoped things would work out according to Soapy's plans, but was unwilling to take any chances. His mission was to rescue Tommy, and he needed to continue his journey, no matter what happened here.

Ka-pow!

This bullet ricocheted off the rock in front of Soapy, spattering his face with stinging dust. Soapy waved his arms again. He did not want the men to move on, even if it meant taking a bullet. Joe could hear Soapy counting out loud.

"Nine, eight, seven . . ."

Joe was scared for Soapy's life. The sharpshooter had his range now, and it would only take one or two more shots to bring the powder man down.

Soapy counted louder now. "Six, five, four, three, two, one . . ."

Nothing happened.

"Get down, Soapy!" Joe yelled. "He's got you in his sights, sure!"

Whump-ka-bloom!

It seemed to Joe as if the entire world shook from the blast of Soapy's charge. He stared in amazement as the cliff crashed down on the hapless men on the trail. Huge boulders and rocks weighing tons cascaded to the valley below.

Soapy came running up to Joe and hugged Devil around the neck, receiving a nip on the shoulder for his efforts.

"I've still got it, Joe!" he shouted. "I'm still the best powder man in three states!"

They led their mounts back to the trail at the bottom of the ravine and mounted up.

"Let's ride, Joe! Come on, Devil! You're carrying the best powder man in five states, girl. Wha-hoo! Let's head for open pasture!"

"You've got it, Soapy!" Joe yelled. "Only I think you're the best powder man in the whole United States!"

Chapter Twelve

Joe and Soapy were careful to stop every few hours and hide behind some rocks. They would wait and rest, making sure that they were no longer being followed by the mine bosses' posse.

Just before dusk they passed a sign that said, *Idaho Springs—2 miles as the crow flies.*

"Do you suppose we should go on in?" Soapy asked. "It might be best to camp outside town and go in tomorrow."

"I want to go in," Joe said. "I want to find the sheriff and ask him if he knows anything about the rustlers we're after. Maybe he can help us. I'm fairly certain we're still on their trail, but it's rained since they've come this way, and I can't tell how far ahead of us they might be. They can't be too far out, even though we've been slowed down. Driving a herd of cattle and horses, they can only cover about half the ground we can. Come on, let's find the sheriff."

"They may not even *have* a sheriff here," Soapy said. "The only law we had in Lost Gulch was the mine bosses' law. There might not be a real law officer here, either."

"Let's go on in and see," Joe said. "Then we'll decide what to do next."

As they came to the outskirts of the town, which seemed to consist of thirty or more well-framed buildings, they passed a water trough, and decided to stop and let Davey and Devil have a drink.

A wagon was parked nearby, with the back end sitting on the ground, both rear wheels missing. A woman and a young boy of about six sat in the front of the wagon, even though it canted upwards at an awkward angle. Two horses were tethered at a nearby tree, and a lone man struggled to raise the back end of the wagon and move a stone underneath it. He was having no luck, as the wagon weighed more than he could lift.

"Looks like he could use some help," Joe said to Soapy. "Come on, let's lend a hand."

As Joe and Soapy approached, the man stopped what he was doing. His dark eyes narrowed skeptically. He was slightly taller and stouter than Joe.

"Need help?" Joe asked, smiling at the man to show he meant him no harm.

"I might," the man said.

Joe realized the man was wary of them, and so gave them

a non-committal answer. He glanced around and saw two recently mended wheels, one lying on each side of the wagon.

"Break your wheels on some rocks?" Joe asked.

"Yep. Never seen so many stones as there are hereabouts. We were moving at night, so the sun would stay off the Missus, and blamed if we didn't strike a rock as big as I am. Front wheels jumped it, but it cracked both rear wheels near in two when they came up on it."

"Was anybody hurt?" Joe asked.

"Nope. Lucky in that respect. But it's been two days since that happened, and I'm just now getting the wheels fixed."

"Which way are you headed?" Joe asked.

"West. We were trying to make it through the Divide before the snows come up. My Missus is mighty anxious to move out."

"Howdy, ma'am," Joe said, tipping his Stetson to the woman in the wagon.

She did not look toward him nor respond, but put an arm around the boy.

"We aren't allowed to talk to strangers," the young boy said quickly, turning toward Joe. He smiled briefly, then just as quickly turned away.

"Can't say as I blame you," Joe said. "It's hard to find a body one can trust any more." He turned back to the man.

"Let us give you a hand, Mister," Joe said. "Soapy and I will help you get the wheels on her, then we can all be on our way."

"I'd be much obliged, mister. My name's Micah. Thanks for the offer."

Joe and Soapy located a downed tree trunk nearby and pushed one end under the wagon. Micah positioned the stone under the trunk, and Joe and Soapy pried upwards. Once the end was high enough in the air, Micah pushed one wheel over the axle. As Joe and Soapy continued holding up the back of the wagon, Micah ran to the other side and pushed on the other wheel.

Joe and Soapy helped him cap off the wheels and they were finished.

"Thanks," Micah said. "If there's any way I can repay you, let me know. We don't have any money, but if you can think of something, ask. I could never have put those wheels on by myself."

"Are you homesteaders?" Joe asked. "Because it's probably too late to make it through the passes before winter hits. You'd best try to find a place to stay till spring."

Micah wiped his brow. "Yep. I was feeling that way, myself. But the Missus wants to go on and try it. I guess we will."

"Good luck," Joe said. "And there is one way you can help us out."

"Oh? How?"

"Have you seen a big herd of cattle run through these parts recently? Heading north?"

"Yesterday," Micah said. "A group passed through here yesterday. They didn't even offer to help us out one little bit. They had horses *and* cattle. They were a mean-looking bunch, too. Scared the Missus pretty good just to glance on 'em. I sure hope you two fellers aren't planning on joining up with the likes of them."

"Not hardly," Joe said. "We're chasing them. Most of those horses and most of the cattle were stolen from the Summerlin ranch, where I'm foreman. They took Missus Summerlin's son, too. Those horse thieves kidnapped the boy."

"Hmm." Micah scratched his chin. "There was a boy with them, looked to be around ten or twelve years old. They called him their 'wild 'un.' I figured he really was a wild boy. One of those unfortunates reared in the woods by wolves, or some such. His clothes were all torn and tattered, and he didn't speak a word. He did all their chores, watering the horses and giving them rubdowns. Soon as he finished, they moved on up the trail."

"You say this was yesterday?" Joe asked.

"Yep. Early morning."

"Your information has repaid us just fine for helping with the wagon, Micah. Thanks. I—"

"Are you Joe?" the boy in the wagon asked.

Chills ran up and down Joe's spine. How had this boy known his name? He could not recall telling it to them.

He nodded. "Why, yes. I am. Have you heard my name before?"

"Nope. The 'wild 'un' scratched you a message, though. In the dirt. Over there." The boy pointed to a cleared area some twenty paces away.

Joe ran over to it and saw the message etched in the dirt. He read it aloud, so everyone could hear.

" 'Joe. I am okay. I know you are coming after me. Please hurry. Your friend, Tommy.' "

Joe and Soapy bade farewell to Micah and his family, tipping their hats as they rode on into town. Micah's wife never said a word to them, but this was not uncommon, and neither of the two men took it personally.

Joe was pleased with the town of Idaho Springs. It was not just a run-down mining camp, but an actual town, with stores, a carpenter's shop, and a good-sized livery. There was only one street, and the buildings were lined up along both sides of it for several hundred paces. At the far, northern end, about a mile distant, the base of a mountain rose upwards, like a giant watch tower guarding the town.

The street was busy, even though it was nearly dark, with both people and horses milling about. Joe was also pleased to note that the appearance of two strangers did not seem to bother the townsfolk. He asked a man where the sheriff's office might be, and was directed to a building in the center of the block on the right-hand side.

"If you can read," the man said, "it's got the word SHER-IFF written in big, bold letters above the door. If you can't read, which is likely the case around here, there's a picture of a tin star, too. Good day to you, gentlemen."

Joe tipped his hat to the man and he and Soapy made their way down the street. When they pulled up in front of the sheriff's office, they saw that there was a lantern burning inside, which meant it was occupied. They tethered Devil and Davey to the hitching post outside and stepped up on the wooden sidewalk.

"I've never seen such nice sidewalks," Joe said to Soapy, stomping on the boards several times to test them out. "These are at least five feet wide and run both sides of the street. This is a high-class town, Soapy." He jumped up and down again.

"Whoa, Joe! Whoa!" Soapy called out, putting a hand on Joe's arm. "Don't ever jump up and down on a wood sidewalk. Never!"

"Why not?"

"Look yonder." Soapy pointed to the boards several feet away. A wasp lit on the top of the board, crawling around to the underside.

"Oh," Joe said. He did not jump any more. "Wasps. I guess they make their paper nests under the boards because they're protected from the rain there."

"You got it, Joe. Just don't jump."

Just as Joe was about to reach for the door, two men bounded out of the office. They sidestepped Joe, but nearly knocked Soapy to the sidewalk.

"Watch where you're standing, old-timer!" the taller of the two men yelled at Soapy. Both men had enormous mustaches, and both wore badges. The taller man's badge identified him as the sheriff, while the badge of the shorter man showed he was a deputy.

"I ain't no older than you, bub!" Soapy answered. He pushed his chest up to the taller man, angry that he had been yelled at. He expected an apology.

"Look here, old-timer," the sheriff said. "I'm the law here. Name's Sheriff Matterson. You had best mind your manners while you're in my town."

"He didn't mean any harm, Sheriff," Joe said, trying to defuse the situation. "He was just—"

"And who the blazes are you, cowboy?" the sheriff asked, standing up on his toes so he would be as tall as Joe. "Did I ask you to stick your busybody nose in this business?"

"My name's Joe Weaver, Sheriff. And we are here on a mission of dire need. We seek your help. We're chasing after some horse thieves who have been through your area recently. We'd be much obliged for some help."

The sheriff backed up a step, eyeing Joe and Soapy suspiciously. He rested his right hand on his revolver.

This was not the response Joe was hoping to receive.

"You two hombres look kind of familiar to me," the sheriff said. He turned to his deputy. "How about you, Wallace? You recognize either of these two strangers?"

Deputy Wallace shook his head, but he, too, placed a hand on his gun grip.

"Either of you two ever been in Lost Gulch?" the sheriff asked.

Joe suddenly had butterflies in his stomach. "Uh, no, Sheriff. Not us. We're from the Summerlin ranch, south of Lost Gulch."

"Deputy Wallace?" the sheriff said. "Why don't you run back inside and get me that telegraph from Lost Gulch. The one that described a horse thief that caused such a ruckus there recently."

"The telegram only described one feller," Deputy Wallace said, looking toward Soapy. "It said he was an old guy."

"I know. But that don't mean a hill of pinto beans. There's always more than one feller involved. Haven't I taught you anything? Get the telegram. Seems to me it described the old guy as having some fingers missing. Go get it, Deputy."

Deputy Wallace turned and ran back inside the office.

"You fellers just wait right where you are," Sheriff Matterson said. "Let's see if we can't clear this matter up before you run off somewhere else."

Joe glanced toward Soapy and noticed he had his left hand stuck down behind his belt, where his fingers could not be counted.

"We're really in a hurry, Sheriff," Joe said. "We aren't horse thieves, we're chasing *after* horse thieves. Honest."

Joe, very slowly, turned to walk away. He did not want to make the sheriff jumpy, so all of his moves were slow and calculated. He hoped that he and Soapy could simply leave, unmolested.

"Hold on, boys!" the sheriff said loudly, pulling his .45. "I got a feeling that *you* two are the horse thieves. You boys reach for the sky and hope you can grab onto a cloud, because that's the only hope you got of getting out of here."

The deputy ran back outside, clutching the telegram. "It says he's short," he said, almost out of breath. "And he's missing two fingers on his left hand."

Joe began jumping up and down.

"What the blazes are you doing?" the sheriff asked.

"Trying to catch hold of one of those clouds, Sheriff," Joe said. "Come on, Soapy. Give me a hand."

Soapy looked at Joe as if he was crazy.

Joe pointed to the sidewalk.

Soapy got the message, and he, too, began jumping up and down.

"You fellers quit that jumping," the sheriff said, reading over the telegram to double check what his deputy had told him. "Stop it. Right now."

"Jump, Soapy!" Joe called out. "Jump high. Jump hard. Jump for all you're worth, Soapy!"

The sheriff looked down at the sidewalk.

"No, you fools!" he shouted. "Don't jump! No!"

Joe heard a buzzing sound and glanced downward. Angry flying insects began coming up between the gaps in the boards.

"Quit your jumping!" the sheriff screamed. "You're gonna make the yaller bees mad as hornets!"

Yaller bees? Joe wondered. *Oh. He means yellow jackets. The little bees with stings that hurt worse than wasps.*

As Joe watched, hundreds of yellow jackets who had built their hive beneath the sidewalk came boiling through the boards.

"Run for your lives!" Sheriff Matterson yelled, forgetting that the two men standing in front of him might be horse thieves.

"Yaller bees!" the sheriff shouted. "Run for it, boys!"

The sheriff and his deputy ran down the sidewalk toward the north, chased by angry yellow jackets.

Joe and Soapy ran, too. They went in the opposite direction, also chased by an angry horde of yellow jackets.

Chapter Thirteen

It took Joe only two seconds to decide to step as softly on the sidewalk boards as possible, even though he was running hard. He realized that there might be more than one yellow jacket nest underneath the boards, plus there were surely many other kinds of wasp nests.

"In here, Joe!" Soapy yelled, stopping abruptly in front of a shop with the door wide open. "The sheriff's running in the other direction, and not looking our way. It's our best chance."

Soapy was breathing hard, and Joe figured they could not keep running on foot and get safely out of town. Sooner or later the sheriff and deputy would mount horses and easily run them down. Besides, Devil and Davy were still tethered to the hitching post in front of the sheriff's office, and Joe was not about to leave Davey in the clutches of strangers again. Soapy was right. This was the best idea for right now.

Joe glanced up at the sign above the entrance—MOSE SMITH, CARPENTER. It seemed as good a place to hide as any, and he rushed inside, Soapy right on his heels.

The carpentry shop was one huge room, about thirty paces square. As soon as Joe got inside, he stopped and stood to one side of the entrance door, searching back down the street for signs of the sheriff.

Soapy got as far as the center of the room when he skidded to a halt in front of something on the sawdust-covered floor. His mouth dropped open and his eyes opened wide in terror.

"Well, knock me over with a feather," Soapy croaked, as he stared around the cavernous room. "Maybe this wasn't such a good idea after all, Joe."

Joe turned and looked around the room for the first time. Chills ran up his spine. Lining all four walls, standing on end, were caskets. There were all kinds and sizes—large, small, ornate, and plain. Joe had never seen so many caskets in one place in his life.

"The man does good work, doesn't he?" Joe said, trying to inject some levity in their situation. "Some of these caskets are genuine works of art. I kind of like that white and gold painted one you're leaning against."

"Akk!" Soapy yelped. He jumped back as if he had been bitten by a rattlesnake. He had not even noticed that he was right next to a casket that was placed on top of two sawhorses. Next to it were three more, sitting on sawhorses in the same manner.

The caskets in the middle of the room all had their lids closed, while most of those leaning against the wall were open. Many were padded inside with velvet cloth, while others were plain, simple wood boxes.

"Uh-oh," Joe said, grabbing Soapy's arm. "Hear that?"

Soapy thought Joe was referring to a noise coming from one of the caskets and he began to shiver. "I don't hear anything, Joe! Let's vamoose!"

"I hear footsteps, Soapy. Coming down the sidewalk. They're heading this way." Joe spun Soapy around and stared into his eyes. "We've got to hide, Soapy."

"Uh . . . you don't mean *hide* where I think you mean *hide*, do you? As in, hide inside one of these bone boxes?" He pointed to one of the empty caskets leaning against the wall and shivered. "I can't do *that*, Joe. I don't even want to be in one of *those* when I pass on to the happy gold-mining camp in the sky."

Joe grabbed Soapy by the shoulders and pushed him toward the nearest open casket. He figured it was not only the nearest, but since it was padded, it would also be the most comfortable.

"It's our only chance, Soapy. Quick! Get in! The footsteps are almost here!"

Soapy closed his eyes and froze. Joe grabbed him, spun him around, and shoved him inside the box. He closed the lid and ran to an open coffin on the adjacent wall. He stepped in it, leaned back, and pulled the lid down. He was just in time.

The sheriff and the deputy, both breathing hard, ran through the open door into the shop. Both came to a stop after only three steps inside.

"Whoa, Sheriff!" Deputy Wallace said. "This is Mose Smith's place. I don't much like being in here. You know I ain't too fond of body crates."

"Those varmints may be hiding in here, Deputy. We gotta search every logical hiding place. You know that."

"Okay, Sheriff, but *you* open the boxes. I don't think I can do it. What if some of 'em have bodies in 'em?"

"Bodies? Can't be. These are all empty caskets, for display. Mose Smith doesn't keep the bodies in here. Once a body is laid to rest in a box, the casket is buried. You know that."

"Wouldn't it be easier to just put a bullet in all the closed ones?" Deputy Wallace asked. "We could shoot dead center. That way we wouldn't have to open them, and anyone who was hiding inside one would be dead. Like he was supposed to be. That sounds like the best plan to me."

"That is one bad plan, Deputy. Mose Smith would get mighty upset with us if we put holes in half his caskets for no good reason. Plus . . . there's that *other* reason you mentioned."

"What other reason?"

"Well . . . what if, just by some terrible coincidence, there *was* a dead body laid up in one of these boxes?"

Deputy Wallace's eyes opened wide. "You promised me that could not happen, Sheriff. You said Mose wouldn't do that."

"Now, Deputy, I did not *promise* you that. I simply said it *shouldn't* be. But maybe, just maybe, Mose got behind. Maybe he didn't have time to plant one of these boxes just yet. I wouldn't want to be responsible for putting an extra bullet hole in somebody's loved one. Would you?"

Deputy Wallace shook his head solemnly.

"So let's just open 'em up and look inside," Sheriff Matterson said. "That way we won't make any mistakes we can't set straight. Okay?"

Deputy Wallace nodded. "Okay, Sheriff. But like I said, *you* do it. *You* open 'em up. I got chill bumps so bad I don't rightly think I can do it."

"I pay you too much," Sheriff Matterson grumbled. "If I got to do all the work, I'm overpaying you."

Sheriff Matterson walked up to the largest coffin on the floor, one that was sitting on top of sawhorses. He drew his revolver, pointed it at the coffin, and yanked the lid open.

"Ahh!" Deputy Wallace screamed.

Blam!

The sheriff fired his gun into the coffin without a second's hesitation. Then, when he realized what he had done, he dropped his shoulders and hung his head.

"Great day in the morning!" Sheriff Matterson cried out. "It's the Widow Anderson! I just shot her dead!"

Deputy Wallace leaned over the coffin and stared at the Widow Anderson. "You sure plugged her, Sheriff, but don't worry too awful much. She was already dead."

"This is impossible!" Sheriff Matterson yelled. "That

can't be the Widow Anderson! She passed away three
weeks ago!"

Deputy Wallace edged toward the door. "I do believe
I'm getting the blazes out of here, Sheriff," he said.

"Why? She dang-sure ain't gonna bite you, Deputy.
She's too dead for that." He looked over the edge of the
coffin. "She didn't have many teeth left, as I recall, anyways."

"Oh, she's dead all right, Sheriff," Deputy Wallace said,
still moving slowly toward the door. "You done put a bullet
in her, to make sure. She's dead twice over!"

Sheriff Matterson slammed the lid down on the coffin
that contained the unfortunate Widow Anderson. "I'm going to have to have a serious talk with Mose Smith about
this, Deputy. We can't have dead folks going unburied
around here. Can you imagine what the townsfolk will say
if they find out about this?"

"Ah-choo!"

The sound of a sneeze erupted from an area near the
wall to the sheriff's left.

"Ahh!" Deputy Wallace screamed. "It's another one who
wasn't buried, Sheriff! Run for it!"

Sheriff Matterson scowled and strode over to one of the
coffins leaning against the wall with the lid closed. He
yanked the lid open and pointed his revolver at Soapy, who
still had his eyes closed.

"This ain't no dead body," Sheriff Matterson said. "Dead
men don't sneeze!"

"That dad-blamed carpenter needs to dust the insides of

his boxes better," Soapy said, opening his eyes. "A man can't breathe proper in there with all that durned sawdust."

"Ah-choo!"

Another sneeze erupted from one of the coffins on the adjacent wall.

"Reach, you sidewinder!" Sheriff Matterson said, pointing his gun at several of the coffins. "Come out or I'll put a bullet in every box on the wall!"

Joe pushed open the cover to his coffin and stepped out of the box. He was pleased to notice that both the sheriff and the deputy were covered with red welts from the yellow jackets.

"You're right, Soapy," Joe said, glancing toward his friend. "The insides of these crates would make a dead man sneeze. I've been holding my breath for the longest." He looked over at the coffin he guessed contained the Widow Anderson.

"I guess the only reason the good Widow didn't sneeze, was because the sheriff plugged her."

"Don't you try to change the subject, horse thief!" Sheriff Matterson yelled. "You fellers are plumb out of luck this time. You got no yaller bees to help you." He rubbed at one of the welts on his neck.

"I'm gonna see to it that you pay for these stingers, too. Get their guns, Deputy."

Deputy Wallace took Soapy and Joe's revolvers, sticking them behind his own belt.

"Now, get outside," Sheriff Matterson said. "This place is giving me the creeps. Move! We're gonna lock you two horse thieves up and lose the key."

Joe and Soapy marched outside, followed by the sheriff and the deputy.

Suddenly, a man wearing an enormous sombrero came running up to the sheriff. He had a bundle in his arms, wrapped in a white shawl with fringe on it.

"Sheriff!" the man yelled. "You gotta do something with this baby!"

"Baby?" the sheriff asked, coming to a halt. "What baby?"

"This one," the man said, holding up the bundle. "I found him lying in the middle of the street."

He pushed the bundle in front of the sheriff's nose. "Here! He's all yours."

Joe had not paid much attention to the man when he had first run up to them, but now, he turned and watched with anticipation.

The man with the huge sombrero winked at Joe. It was Chili!

"I can't fool with no baby!" the sheriff yelled at Chili. He holstered his weapon and backed up a step, hoping the man would not just drop the bundle on the ground. "I got a problem with horse thieves, here."

"You are the sheriff, are you not?" Chili asked, still holding the bundle out to him.

The sheriff nodded, but did not take the bundle.

"Then you are the law," Chili said. "An abandoned baby is your responsibility. Here . . ." He pushed the bundle into the sheriff's arms, and the man reluctantly cradled the little shawl-wrapped bundle tightly, afraid he would drop him.

Deputy Wallace, his curiosity getting the best of him, peered over and pulled on the cloth covering the baby's face with his free hand. "I wonder—"

In a flash, the Gila monster hidden behind the white shawl snapped out and bit the unsuspecting sheriff on the tip of his nose.

"Ahh!" Sheriff Matterson screamed, tossing the bundle in the air.

"It's a monster baby!" Deputy Wallace yelled. Without even checking on the two prisoners, the deputy took off running down the street, the sheriff right behind him.

Chili reached out and grabbed the bundle before it hit the ground.

"¡Vamos!" Chili yelled to Joe and Chili. "Let's get out of here while we can."

Leading the way, the bundle held securely in his arms, Chili ran between two buildings toward the safety of the woods beyond.

All three were hidden by the trees before Sheriff Matterson had the sense to stop and turn around, realizing he had been tricked. His prisoners had escaped once again. Now he was mad. Now he was very mad.

Chapter Fourteen

Joe, Soapy, and Chili did not stop running when they reached the woods. They kept on until they knew they were safe. They ran down a small valley, and up the other side, where there were an adequate number of thick trees to hide them from the view of anyone in Idaho Springs.

"Whoa, guys!" Joe finally called out. "We're out of sight, and no one's coming through the brush after us. Let's rest."

All three were breathing hard when they came to a stop. Chili still carried the shawl-wrapped bundle in his arms.

"Thanks, Chili," Joe said, when his breathing had returned to normal. "And give my thanks to El Gato, too."

"El Gato?" Soapy asked. "That's Spanish for *the cat*. I didn't see any cat. You can't have a cat in that shawl. No sheriff would be scared of a cat." He peered intently at the bundle in Chili's arms.

Chili stood a head shorter than Joe, about even with

Soapy, but his arms were thicker than Soapy's legs. He had a huge brown mustache, and still wore his enormous sombrero, painted brightly with cacti and cactus flowers.

It was difficult to glance in Chili's direction and not stare at his large, colorful sombrero.

"This *is* El Gato," Chili said, lightly rocking the bundle in his arms. "He is my pet."

"You got a cat for your pet?" Soapy asked, disdainfully. "I never seen a cat that would allow a man to rock it back and forth like it was a baby. I never seen a cowboy who *wanted* a cat for a pet. What kind of cat is it?"

"El Gato is a very special cat," Chili said, grinning mischievously. "Listen closely and you can hear him purr."

"Sss! Sss!"

Soapy could hear the animal in Chili's arms making a noise, but it did not sound like a purr to him.

"Let me see that rascal," Soapy said, pulling back on the white shawl. "He purrs the loudest of any cat I ever—"

"Akk!" Soapy jumped backwards, nearly stumbled, then regained his footing. He wiped his brow and grinned at Chili.

"No wonder that smart-alecky sheriff feller jumped," Soapy said. "That ain't no baby, and it ain't no cat, either. It's a dad-blamed thunder lizard!"

"Ah," Chili said. "So you know *el lagarto del trueno*, the lizard of the thunder?"

"Yep," Soapy said. "That's just a fancy name for a dad-blamed Gila monster." He looked hard at Chili. "You're a crazy man to keep a Gila for a pet, the way I see it. You're crazy as a cactus buzzard!"

"I apologize for not introducing you two," Joe said, grinning at them both. "Soapy, this is Chili, and Chili, this is Soapy."

The two men shook hands, though Soapy made sure he kept out of El Gato's biting range.

Joe turned to Chili. "I met Soapy down at Lost Gulch," he said. He turned to Soapy.

"Chili is my foreman at the ranch, Soapy. He's also the cook—the best cook in three states, bar none."

The two nodded to each other.

"Let's keep moving," Joe said. "If the sheriff picks up our trail, we don't want him to walk right in on us."

Chili uncovered El Gato and gently scratched the huge lizard's pink, yellow, and black head as the three walked along a narrow trail. The lizard was over two-and-a-half feet long, with large, powerful claws, and jaws as massive as a man's fist.

"Won't he bite?" Soapy asked Chili. "I've never seen one that didn't bite."

"Oh, he bites," Chili said somberly. "But only the bad guys."

"You make sure then, Chili, that El Gato knows I'm a good guy. Okay?"

"Okay."

"Look," Joe said, pointing to the north. "There's a mine shaft up there, on the side of the mountain, at the far end of town. Let's head for it. We'll have shelter and a chance to rest and regroup."

Chili and Soapy agreed and the three turned toward the

north. They were careful as they walked to keep behind shrubbery, since the town was only about a thousand paces away, and they might be seen if they were in the open.

"How the Sam Hill did you end up with a Gila for a pet, anyways?" Soapy asked. He became brave enough to walk beside Chili, where he could see the lizard close up. He did not reach over and pet him, however, as Chili was doing.

"Not many folks would pick a feisty lizard to be their companion," Soapy said.

"I was in Arizona, Soapy," Chili said. "About two years ago. I was searching for saguaro blossoms to put into my famous Cactus Blossom Soup."

"Famous soup?" Soapy asked. "I never heard of a soup being famous. I don't care much for soup, famous or not. Had to eat tater soup too many times to keep from starving. I never choose soup if I can help it."

"Chili's soup," Joe said, as they continued to walk, "is known far and wide, Soapy. And not because of the cactus blooms, either. It's because he puts so many hot chilies in it, a man's stomach near about lights on fire!"

"Pay Joe no attention," Chili said. He stepped carefully over a rotting tree trunk. "My Cactus Blossom Soup is mild. It's my Caramba Soup you want to avoid, if you don't like hot peppers. But let me continue with my story, please."

Chili scratched El Gato and went on with his tale, as the three men continued to make their way north.

"I had ridden up to a large group of saguaro cacti, and was examining them from my horse, when a shot rang out behind me. Suddenly, my horse dropped dead beneath me."

"I pure despise a man who'll shoot a feller's horse," Soapy said.

"Me, too," Chili agreed. "And when I finally stood up, the hombre had *me* in his sights. He was ten paces away, pointing the barrel of a Colt .45 right between my eyes."

"Watch out for this branch," Soapy said, as he pulled a limber cedar branch out of Chili's way.

"I asked the man who he was," Chili continued, bending down under the branch, "and why he was doing this to me. He never said a word. He pulled back the hammer on his revolver, and I heard it click into place. I looked up to heaven, because I knew this was the end. I was in the middle of the desert, standing in front of a man who was about to shoot me. My only companions were the saguaro cactuses. They, too, seemed to reach into the sky with their limbs. It was as if we had all reached the end. I was as good as dead."

For the next fifteen minutes they traversed a steep incline, as they closed in on the mouth of the mine. During all of this time, Chili did not continue with his story. He looked over at Soapy every minute or so, to see how the man was reacting to his silence.

"Well, tarnation, man!" Soapy said with exasperation as they walked the last few steps to the mine. "What happened? You can't just stop telling a story like that, right in the middle! Did the varmint kill you or not?"

Chili grinned, pleased to see that he had not lost the ability to make his listener want to hear the rest of the story.

"Do you see any holes in my head, Soapy?" Chili asked.

"Remember? I told you the gun was pointed directly at my head."

"You could have ducked!" Soapy said. "Besides, you might have a whole head full of holes, for all I know. Maybe you got 'em covered with that big-as-Texas sombrero. Any man who keeps a Gila lizard for a pet, *does* have holes in his head, I would say." Soapy swatted at a fly buzzing around his head.

"Now, get on with it, Chili," he said. "Tell us what happened."

They were now on level ground near the mine, so the three men stopped and Chili waved his hands dramatically, as he continued with his tale.

"The man was incredibly steady. The barrel of his gun, pointed directly at my head, did not waver the slightest little bit. Not a bit! But suddenly, the man's horse reared in the air. He fired the revolver, but it was too late. The bullet went wide of its mark, shooting harmlessly into the sky. The man was thrown from his horse. *Whoosh!* And he crashed to the earth, head first. *Whump! Crack!* When the man hit the ground, I could hear the bones in his neck break, easily as the branch on a dead tree."

"So you got on his horse and rode off, huh?" Soapy asked. "End of story?"

"No, Soapy. Not quite." Chili took off his sombrero, wiped the sweat from his forehead, then replaced the hat.

"His horse bolted once more, then turned, and ran away, as if he were running from the Devil himself."

"Why'd he run like that?" Soapy asked.

"Something scared him, Soapy. Something made the horse rear up and toss his rider, then that same something scared the horse so bad he took off running for the Rio Grande."

"What in tarnation was it?" Soapy asked. He was getting tired of having to make Chili continue with the story.

"I saw a sudden movement to my left," Chili said. "A sidewinder! The rattlesnake was skittering across the sand right at me, as if he hadn't already scared enough folks to death. Now it was *my* turn!"

Chili paused, and nodded toward the inside of the mine. "Looks pretty good, Joe. Want me and Soapy to have a look inside?"

"Look inside?" Soapy yelled. "I'm gonna chase you inside, if you don't get on with the telling of that story! Quit stalling, durn your hide. Tell me what happened next. Did the sidewinder bite you?"

"Ohh, that skittering snake," Chili said. "He moved to the left, he moved to the right. I was so afraid I could not run. I was frozen. I was a dead man. The snake came right up to my boots, flicked his evil tongue at them, and reared back his head, making ready for the strike. Then . . . *whack!*"

Chili shook his head somberly, staring down at the ground. He did not say a word. He squinted his eyes up at Soapy, trying to see if the suspense was too much for him. There was nothing Chili loved better than to make his stories as suspenseful as possible.

This time Soapy remained quiet. He was tired of Chili playing games with him, and was determined to out-wait him. He figured Chili wanted to tell the story more than Soapy wanted to hear it, and sooner or later would get on with it.

"The mine looks like it's been used recently," Joe said, eager to get on to the real task at hand. "Let's look inside."

Neither Soapy nor Chili made a move. Neither one spoke. Both were set on not being the first to say a word.

Joe felt this could get very tiring, very fast.

"You two are about as stubborn as two mules," he said. "Maybe we should—"

"Reach for the sky!" Sheriff Matterson's voice rang out from behind them. "You three horse thieves are surrounded! We've got you outnumbered, too."

Joe, Chili, and Soapy slowly raised their hands.

Joe winced. They were fifteen paces from the protection of the mine shaft. If only they had gone on inside, instead of standing around out here!

"How did you find us?" Joe asked, as Sheriff Matterson, Deputy Wallace, and two other armed men stepped out from behind nearby shrubs and walked toward them.

"You dumb fellers," Sheriff Matterson said, "walked right up to us, actually. We saw you coming a while back, and hid in the bushes."

"Why were you waiting for us at this old mine shaft?" Joe asked.

"Mine shaft?" the sheriff said. "This ain't no mine shaft. This is our jail!"

"Uh-oh," Chili said, gazing around somberly. "It seems, Joe, we have jumped from the pot right into the frying pan!"

Chapter Fifteen

Sheriff Matterson and his deputies herded Joe, Soapy, and Chili deeper into the mine shaft that had been converted into a jail. They took Joe and Soapy's empty gun belts, and Chili's gun and belt. None of the deputies bothered to try and take the shawl-covered Gila monster away from Chili.

"Don't you want to see the baby?" Chili asked the deputies.

"Keep him!" Sheriff Matterson yelled. "If you fellers get hungry, you can always eat grilled lizard! Ha!"

Chili did not laugh. He never laughed when people made jokes about eating his Gila monster.

The deputies quickly patted down Joe and Soapy for hidden weapons, but none of them approached Chili. They were not about to search a man carrying a live Gila monster.

"Search him!" Sheriff Matterson commanded.

"But Sheriff—" Deputy Wallace started.

"No buts! Search him. Do it from behind if you're so all-fired scared of a dad-gummed lizard. Do it!"

Deputy Wallace stood behind Chili and patted him down as fast as he could, immediately jumping to one side when he was finished. Chili grinned with glee at the man.

Joe noticed that Sheriff Matterson was not brave enough, himself, to search Chili. Joe watched everything with intensity. He had to admit that this was a great location for a jail. They went about twenty paces into the mouth of the mine before they came to the bars, stretched across a section of the cave that was about fifteen feet wide and ten feet high. In the center of these bars a door was hinged to a steel column. The bars could not be seen from the outside, and those locked behind them could not see anything but the sky beyond the mouth of the mine entrance. This would not be a very nice place to spend any length of time. Joe decided that he would not be behind these bars any longer than necessary.

He also noticed that there was no furniture on the other side of the bars. There were no tables, chairs, or bunk beds, just bare rock walls, a rock ceiling, and a rock floor.

Deputy Wallace locked the door behind the three, tossing in two blankets just before the door clanged shut.

"Only got two," Deputy Wallace said. "You'll have to share."

"Yep," Sheriff Matterson said, staring coldly at the three men on the other side of the bars. "A mine shaft with bars is just about the best doggone jail that can be bought." He laughed.

"It don't cost nothing, actually, because a bunch of fellers already dug it out, searching for gold. Ha-ha! You fellers can wander through that shaft all you want—we didn't board it up at the other end. It just goes and goes. I heard there are about twenty miles of tunnels running through this mountain, all starting right here. Of course, if you get lost, us setting out water and food for you on this end won't help you much, will it? You fellers think about that before you mosey off down the mine shaft. Ha!"

"Last six prisoners we put in here disappeared," Deputy Wallace said. "If you men run across their bodies, how about pulling them back here so we can bury them proper!"

"You fellers can hunt up all the yaller bees and monster babies you want," the sheriff said. "They can't help you in there! No, sir! Nobody's *ever* broke out of *this* jail!"

"We haven't done anything wrong, Sheriff," Joe said, hoping the man would finally listen to him. "We're not the bad guys."

"I reckon we'll just let the court decide your innocence, buster," the sheriff said, grinning wickedly. "In Idaho Springs, we let the court tell us if a man is good or bad."

"A court?" Joe asked, feeling a sense of relief. He had more faith in a court than he did the impulsive sheriff.

"With a judge?" Joe asked. "And a jury?"

"Yep!" Sheriff Matterson said, laughing loudly. "Of course, you'll still have me to deal with."

"What do you mean?" Joe asked.

"I'm the judge, here, too! And my deputies, all three of 'em, are the jury!" The sheriff waited for the three deputies to stop laughing before he went on.

"The trial will be held tomorrow morning, at sunrise." He grinned as he watched the crestfallen expression on Joe's face. "I wouldn't bet on being let go, if I was one of you fellers. You'll be sentenced to ten years' hard labor, or my name ain't Matterson!"

"Hey!" Soapy called out. "What are you gonna do with our guns?"

"They'll be right out here, fellers," the sheriff said. "They'll be hanging from a tree branch, like dead possums waiting for the buzzards to land. Once we hang 'em up, they're public property and anyone who comes along is welcome to them."

"But someone will steal them," Soapy replied. "They ain't public property."

"So what? You fellers won't ever have a use for them again. Not ever!"

The sheriff strode off, laughing loudly, with two of the deputies. Only Deputy Wallace remained behind.

"Ten years?" Joe asked the deputy. "In here? He's going to sentence us to ten years' hard labor stuck in an abandoned mine shaft?"

"Oh, no," Deputy Wallace said. "He means ten years' hard labor working on the spur line."

"What spur line?" Joe asked.

"The one the railroad's putting in, up the other side of the mountain." Deputy Wallace pointed up the mountain behind them.

"They found gold up there last year," the deputy said. "But there's no practical way to work it, then get the rock down here to be taken to the stamp mill at Lost Gulch."

Joe swallowed hard. It sounded to him as if the same men who owned Lost Gulch were the ones building the railroad spur line up the mountain. The situation was beginning to look very hopeless to him.

"Yep," the deputy went on. "It's hard work putting a spur line up a mountain, fellers. Takes a lot of men. We rent all our prisoners to the railroad bosses, who'll work you men pretty much to death. You'll be in leg irons *and* wrist irons, chipping away at this old mountain with shovels and picks."

"That's not legal!" Joe said. "You can't rent prisoners out to the railroad."

"We do it, legal or not. Who's gonna complain? Besides, it all works out for the best. Our town gets the money for renting you out, we don't have to feed and clothe you while you're serving your sentence for being horse thieves, and the spur line gets built."

"It sounds dangerous to me," Joe said. "How do they expect men to work safely on a mountainside when they're chained up?"

The deputy laughed. "Oh, it *is* dangerous. About as dangerous a job as a man can have. There's dynamite going off all the time, rock slides, and giant trees falling over. In the last two months, we've lost seven prisoners up there, one way or another. Of course, the mine bosses are fair. They're as fair as can be. They continue to pay the rental on the dead men, until their original sentence runs out. That sounds about as good a deal as I've ever heard of. Don't you think so?"

Joe grabbed the bars and shook his head. "We aren't horse thieves, deputy! You have to believe me!"

"I have to go," Deputy Wallace said. "I'll bring you fellers some beans and coffee in the morning. Sleep well, 'cause once you get on the spur line, there isn't much sleeping. It's *bang-bang-bang*, pounding in railroad spikes, all day long, and into the night. Ha! Be careful, fellers. After they set off a dynamite charge to move some rock out of the way, it's powerful easy to get caught up in a mud slide. Ha! Once you get pushed down the mountain by a few tons of rock and Douglas firs, you won't be eager to steal horses again! Not ever!"

Deputy Wallace laughed several times and jingled the keys in front of the three men, taunting them. He stuck the keys in his pocket and walked off.

"José?" Chili asked somberly.

"Yes? What, Chili?" Joe was pushing his brain, trying to come up with a solution to their dilemma. He did not want to make idle chit-chat.

"It looks, José, like we have jumped again. This time we have jumped out of the frying pan and into the fire!"

"Yeah, Chili," Joe said softly. "We've gone from one bad place to another, all right. But don't give up, guys. We'll find a way out of this, yet. We have to find a way out. Remember, we haven't even found Tommy. Our fate is linked to his fate. We'll make it. Just don't give up."

"But won't they be so far ahead of us, we'll never catch up?" Chili asked.

Joe shook his head. "Not really. They can't drive the herd at night, and even during the day, they can't make good time with so many animals to keep track of. We'll catch up to them."

"No matter about how slow they go," Soapy said sadly, "Chili is right. We're smack in the middle of the fire. The problem is that once in the fire, it's kind of hard to just jump out. And we have to get out in order to catch up to the rustlers."

Joe, Chili, and Soapy sat on the cold rock floor of the mine for fifteen minutes without saying a word. Each was deep in thought, trying to figure a way out of their seemingly hopeless situation. El Gato rested quietly in Chili's lap, oblivious to the problems facing the three men.

Joe had no desire to test the sheriff's words that there was no way out of the mine shaft except through the bars. He sighed. He had been on the wrong end of far too many mine shafts recently. He did not care if he never saw another mine shaft as long as he lived.

Joe knew that Tommy was probably going through similar emotions right now. Like Joe, Tommy must feel helpless, and the situation would seem hopeless. At least Joe had the company of two friends at this moment. Tommy had no one.

Soapy stood up and began pacing back and forth, his eyes hard on Chili.

"Well?" Soapy finally said, coming to a stop in front of

Chili, who was still sitting on the floor. "Well?" Soapy repeated, staring at Chili with disdain.

"Well, what?" Chili asked.

"Well," Soapy replied, hands on his hips. "I reckon, now that we've got a heap of time on our hands, that you can finish that story you were telling us."

"What story?" Chili looked up at Soapy with mirth in his eyes.

"You know durn well what story! The one where the rattlesnake is about to bite the daylights out of you, that's what! In fact, I'm going to pull for the rattler. I hope he *did* bite you. How about them apples?"

"Well, amigo, I am sorry to say that your hopes were not granted. As you will hear, shortly, when I finish telling you this amazing, true story."

"I'm waiting."

"And I am granting your request, Señor Soapy." Chili took a deep breath, made sure that both Joe and Soapy were paying attention, then began his story in earnest.

"I was paralyzed when the rattler made ready to strike. I could not move. He had me hypnotized, staring me down with his evil, slotted eyes. The sidewinder slithered closer, closer. And all of a sudden, from around the back side of the nearest saguaro cactus, huge jaws snapped out and sliced the sidewinder in two!"

Chili paused, to catch his breath.

"Flip-flip-flip! The two halves of the snake bounced across the sand. The half of the snake with the head came flipping my way, the still-snapping jaws opening and closing, even as the snake died! The snake was hoping, with luck, to seize upon the object of its demise and cause it, too, to die!" Chili sighed. "But it was a useless effort. El Gato, my thunder lizard, was too smart for the snake's dying efforts. El Gato snapped his jaws out and swallowed the half of the snake with the tail, rattles and all. He gobbled it down, and sat, watching as the headed section slowly came to a stop. The snake was finished. El Gato turned his massive head and stared up, into my eyes. I leaned over and scratched his head, like this."

The lizard, still in Chili's lap, looked up with adoration into the eyes of the man who was scratching his head.

"He still loves for me to scratch him," Chili said. "Just as I did that day he saved my life in the desert. We have been best of friends ever since, and not a day goes by that I do not scratch his head. Not a single day."

"Well, that's a pretty fair story," Soapy said. "Kind of anti-climactic, if you ask me. For a real good story, the snake should have bit someone. It does remind me of the time I was in southern Arizona, about four years ago. I was cornered up a tree by *three* rattlers, each one as big around as a man's leg. Those vicious rascals—"

"Hold on!" Joe said loudly, interrupting Soapy. "Let's stop this story-telling, men. We need to solve our present dilemma, not re-hash old ones. If we just sit around telling stories, tomorrow morning will be here before we know it, and then we'll be in deep trouble."

Chili nodded and stood up, placing El Gato gently on the ground.

"Didn't you tell me you were a powder man, Soapy?" Chili asked.

Soapy smiled. "I reckon I did, because I am."

"Well," Chili continued, "I have never known a real powder man who did not always carry the makings of an explosion somewhere on his person. I have never met a real powder man who could not blow things up any time he felt the urge. No matter where he was, and no matter what the situation was."

"Heh-heh-heh!" Soapy rocked back and forth on his tip-toes as he laughed. "I told you, I was a real powder man. I meant it, too, bub!"

"Oh, yeah?" Chili pushed up next to Soapy, his face mere inches away. "Let's see, Señor Soapy. Prove it!"

Chapter Sixteen

Soapy went off several paces and began taking off his clothes. He removed his boots, his trousers, and his shirt. He carefully pulled two half-squashed cigars out of his long underwear and put them on the floor of the mine, where he would not step on them.

"I always keep a few of my fuse lighters hidden away," he said. "They're a little flattened, but should be as good as new once they breathe a while."

Soapy stood in front of Joe and Chili, holding his trousers and shirt in his hand, wearing only his socks, his long underwear, and a smile on his face.

"So," he said, glancing at Chili. "You think I ain't a gen-u-ine powder man, huh? Well, I'll show you, bub. I've got blast makings everywhere!"

"You do?" Joe asked, moving closer. "You can make dynamite?"

Soapy shook his head. "Nope. I can't make dynamite. That requires makings I don't carry. But I do have these!"

He rolled the legs of his trousers inside out, revealing a large, flat, cloth bag sewn to each one. Soapy carefully ripped the threads holding the bags to the trousers, and set each one gently on the ground.

"And, I've got these."

Soapy reached inside each boot and carefully removed a cloth bag from each one.

"These double as cushions for my poor, old aching feet," he said, adding the bags to the pile on the rock floor.

Next, Soapy turned the sleeves of his shirt inside out and removed two smaller cloth bags. "Those four bags on the ground are gunpowder," he said. "These here are fuses and matches. Got to have all of these to make any kind of good blast."

He shook his head and grinned at Chili. "And you said I wasn't no powder man! Phooey! You need to eat those words."

"Speaking of eating," Joe said, looking toward Chili. "How about you?"

"Me?" Chili asked. "Me, what? I don't carry gunpowder."

"No, but don't you carry something else?"

"Well, maybe I carry some articles that are necessary for my own craft, which is cooking. But how will these help us?"

"Show us what they are," Joe said. "Then we'll decide if we can use them."

"José. I have nothing that will help."

"Chili, I have known you long enough to know that there are items you *never* leave home without. Show us what you have."

"He ain't got nothing, Joe," Soapy said. "I'm the only one who's going to be able to help us get out of this situation. The only one. Chili ain't worth the salt it takes to jerk beef."

"Not worth salt? I'll show you!" Chili snatched off his sombrero and flipped it over in his hand. He grabbed the sweat band inside the high felt crown, turned it over, and shook the sombrero over the ground. Six small, folded, paper packets, about two inches square, tumbled out onto the rocky surface. Chili held each packet in the air, one at a time.

"Salt, black pepper, mustard powder, dried garlic, dried jalapeño peppers, and dried serrano peppers. Ha!"

Chili held out the packet containing the serrano pepper to Soapy.

"Do you care to take a sniff, Señor Soapy? To see if I am telling you the truth? Some people say the jalapeño is the hottest of the peppers, but I will put my home-grown serranos up against them for blazing heat any day of the week. Have some. Please. Then you can tell us which is the hottest."

Soapy held up a hand and backed up a step.

"Not me, Mister Chili. I don't hanker after hot chilies."

Joe held up his hands. "Enough bickering, you two. Both of you have done just fine. Between Soapy's gunpowder and Chili's peppers, we will have the makings of our escape."

"We will?" Chili asked. "How?"

"I'll show you in just a minute, but we still need one more item. We need casings for our little explosions."

"Casings, I don't have, Joe," Soapy said.

"Me, either," Chili added.

Joe caught sight of the two cigars Soapy had placed on the ground earlier.

"I think you do have casings, Soapy," he said, walking over to the cigars and picking them up. "These!"

Soapy shook his head. "You're welcome to use them, Joe, but we won't get much of a blast. It'll be more like a little *poof*. They aren't rigid enough to blow up much of anything."

"We don't need them to blow up something else," Joe replied. "They just need to explode." He sat on the ground next to El Gato and gently scratched the lizard on the back of his head.

"Between the three of us . . ." he began, then glanced down at El Gato. "Uh, *four* of us, I mean. We will have all the blasting we need."

For the first time in hours, Joe felt a sense of relief. He would find a way to rescue Tommy, no matter what obstacles were put in his way.

In the morning, when the sun finally rose over the low hills in the east, Joe was ready. He stood at the bars to the jail, and spotted the two men coming up the hill from town when they were about three hundred paces off.

"Just two of them," he said to Chili and Soapy, who were sitting together on the rocky floor of the mine telling each other stories. "Everything ready?"

Chili and Soapy nodded gleefully.

"Which two is it?" Chili asked.

"Looks like Deputy Wallace and one of the other deputies. Each one is carrying a sack, and it looks like some kind of chains over Wallace's shoulders. Probably the leg irons. I sure hope my plan works. They'll be here in a jiffy."

Joe looked thoughtfully at Soapy. "The show's all yours, Soapy. Give it to 'em!"

Joe moved to a spot next to the door and sat down, leaning back against the bars of the jail. Chili moved up and sat back down on the other side of the door, placing El Gato by his side and covering him with a blanket. All three were ready as the two deputies neared the jail.

"You fellers up yet?" Deputy Wallace yelled out. "Get up, horse thieves. I got your coffee and your beans. *And* your leg irons!"

Both deputies laughed loudly at Wallace's little joke, as they opened the sacks and pulled out six tin cups. Deputy Wallace poured coffee into three cups, and the other deputy slopped a spoonful of beans into three cups. Then they handed each prisoner a cup of each.

"This is it?" Joe asked. "You expect us to work at hard labor on the railroad after just coffee and a few cold beans?"

Deputy Wallace laughed. "We don't aim to spend a lot of money feeding prisoners."

He searched the jail with curious eyes. "Where's that big old lizard? I got a few beans for him, too. You fellers didn't get hungry and eat him, did you?"

Both deputies laughed.

"He ran off into the mine somewhere," Chili said, glancing down to be sure El Gato was still covered with the blanket. "He's been gone since last night."

"Good. That means more beans left over for the three of you. Hurry up and eat. We gotta move you to the spur line, pronto!"

As the other deputy held a gun on the three, Deputy Wallace unlocked the door to the prison.

"Come out one at a time," he said, pointing to Soapy. "You first, old-timer. And no tricks, either."

Soapy held up both hands and walked outside, coming to a stop in front of Deputy Wallace, who leaned down to attach leg irons to him.

"First the legs, then the wrists," Deputy Wallace said. "You can't get in trouble *then*."

"Hold on," Soapy said. "Before you lock up my hands, I'd like to have one last smoke. Once I get to the railroad, I won't have the time."

"Smoke?" Deputy Wallace asked, looking up. "I ain't going to give you one of my smokes."

"I got my own," Soapy said, reaching into his shirt pocket. He pulled out two cigars and a match. "I'll smoke one of these, if you don't mind."

Deputy Wallace jumped up and snatched the cigars out of Soapy's hand.

"Well, doggone it, I *do* mind." He looked the cigars over with eager eyes, sticking one in his mouth and handing the other to his partner. "I do believe that *we* will smoke these cigars, old-timer."

"Hey!" Soapy complained. "Those are *mine*."

"You're a jail bird, old-timer. You don't own anything. Everything you've got belongs to me. Do you understand?"

"Yes, sir," Soapy said. He struck the match on the bottom of his boot and held it out. Both deputies leaned forward to let him light their cigars.

"Pretty good cigars, old-timer," Deputy Wallace said, leaning down to finish putting the leg irons on Soapy.

Both men took long draws on their cigars.

Pop!

One cigar exploded, showering serrano chili powder over Deputy Wallace's face.

Whop!

The second cigar blew up, spraying hot chili powder over the other man's face.

"Aiiee!" both deputies screamed.

"Help! I'm blinded!" Deputy Wallace yelled.

By the time the deputies realized what was happening, Joe and Chili had bounded out of the jail and pinned them to the ground.

They put both men in leg irons and wrist manacles and pushed them into the jail, locking the door behind them.

"Give us something for our eyes!" Deputy Wallace yelled. "They burn like the devil! Give us something."

"Here," Soapy said, passing a tin cup to Deputy Wallace,

who took it eagerly, even though he could barely see. He immediately tossed the contents over his face.

"What is this?" he yelled. "I wanted water."

"Well, we don't like to spend a lot of money on prisoners," Soapy said. "So all you're gonna get is beans. Hope you enjoy them."

Chili dumped one of the cloth bags and put El Gato inside.

Joe grabbed the other bag and put the extra set of irons and manacles in it.

"Why are you bringing those?" Soapy asked.

"I'll find a use for them," Joe said in a low voice, so the deputies could not overhear. "Come on. Let's grab our holsters and guns and head for town."

"Town?" Soapy whispered. "I thought we were heading for the railroad to rescue Tommy."

"We are," Joe said. "But first, we rescue Davey and Devil. We're not leaving them behind."

"How about Cortabolsas?" Chili asked. "He is in town, too. I tied him and the wagon next to Davey. I can't leave Cortabolsas in Idaho Springs."

Joe nodded. "Him, too. Let's go."

The three retrieved their guns and holsters and set out for town, Joe carrying his bag, and Chili carrying the one with El Gato in it.

"Hey!" Deputy Wallace called out. "Don't leave us in here!"

Joe stopped and looked back. "Why not?" he asked with a smile. "You didn't mind leaving us in there all night."

"Yeah, but that big lizard is in here somewhere!"

"Yes, he is," Chili said, grinning wickedly. "And remember that he is a sneaky lizard, too. His favorite joke is to crawl up to a man while he is sleeping, when he least expects it, and bite off one of his fingers, or his toes. Sometimes, he bites off a nose! *Adiós,* deputies. Don't fall asleep. If you do, when you wake up, you might not be all there! Ha!"

Chapter Seventeen

As the three men walked down the hill toward town, they could hear dynamite blasts in the distance.

"Suppose that's from the spur line?" Soapy asked. "It sounds like it's coming from the mountain, on the other side."

"My guess is that you're right," Joe said. "We'll find out soon."

There were few people up and about this early, and the three were able to sneak alongside the carpenter's store, emerging on Main Street, without meeting a single person.

"There they are," Joe said softly, stopping the group. "Right where we left them."

He pointed down the street, where Davey, Devil, and Cortabolsas were still tied to the hitching post in front of the sheriff's office.

"Those varmints!" Soapy said. "That means our poor animals haven't been fed or watered since yesterday! How can that sheriff be so callous?"

"He treats his animals like he treats his prisoners, Soapy," Joe said. "Come on. It's too late to fret over them. Let's mount up and ride out of here."

The three made it to the horses without incident. Joe hugged Davey, Soapy let Devil nip him on the shoulder, and Chili apologized profusely to Cortabolsas for ignoring him overnight. Chili promised him water and oats just as soon as possible.

"What the tarnation is going on out here?" Sheriff Matterson yelled, as he came running out of his office. His face was still swollen from the yellow jacket stings.

"Who are you men? Leave those horses be! Those are property of the Sheriff's Office."

Joe realized that the sheriff did not recognize them. He probably could not see well because of the stings near his eyes, plus he had no reason to think that the prisoners could have escaped. They should have been on their way to the railroad camp by now. Joe slowly let his hand fall toward his revolver.

The sheriff pushed his way past Cortabolsas, shoving the horse roughly.

He stopped abruptly, three paces from Joe, recognition finally dawning on his face.

"Why . . . you're one of the horse thieves! How did you get here? Where's Deputy Wallace?" The sheriff reached for his weapon, several beats ahead of Joe.

His holster was empty.

"What the—? What happened to my gun?" Flustered, the sheriff spun around, facing Cortabolsas.

Held tightly in the horse's teeth was the sheriff's gun.

Joe laughed and pointed his own weapon at the sheriff. "It seems as if Cortabolsas does not like the way you've been treating him, Sheriff."

"Cortabolsas?" the sheriff asked, staring at his revolver dangling in the horse's mouth. "Who is Cortabolsas?"

"My horse!" Chili said, joining in the laughter. He took the gun from Cortabolsas's mouth and stuck it behind his own belt. "His name is Cortabolsas, Spanish for 'the pickpocket.' Wouldn't you say he has been rightly named, Sheriff?"

"And now," Joe said, tossing the leg irons and wrist manacles on the ground in front of the sheriff, "it is time for you to get into your costume, Sheriff. Please put these chains on yourself. Then we can go to the Costume Ball."

Sheriff Matterson glowered, unable to speak, as he put himself in irons.

"Now what?" he said, after he clasped the wrist manacles on his arms. "You can't exactly hide the fact that you're kidnapping me, you know? When the townspeople see me in chains, you won't get very far."

Joe grinned. "Soapy? Do you remember your hiding place, yesterday?"

Soapy nodded, unsure what Joe was going to request.

"You and Chili go get one, while I keep an eye on the sheriff."

Joe busied himself tying a bandanna around the sheriff's mouth, as Soapy led Chili down the sidewalk.

"Don't worry, Sheriff," Joe said, once the gag was tied tightly. "You'll be nice and comfortable. I promise you."

In less than three minutes, Soapy and Chili returned, carrying one of the plain wooden coffins from the carpenter's shop. They placed it on the wagon, then helped Joe put the sheriff inside.

"A good place for a bad man," Chili said, closing the lid. He climbed into the wagon's seat and took the reins to Cortabolsas.

Joe and Soapy mounted up, and just as they were about to leave, two young boys walked up to them, curious as to what they were doing. One boy looked to be about eight, Joe figured, and the other around ten. Both had long, unkempt, blond hair, and neither had washed their faces in a day or so.

"Who died?" the ten-year-old asked.

"Shouldn't you be eating breakfast somewhere?" Soapy asked. "Somewhere else?"

"Or in school?" Joe added.

"Naw," the younger boy said. "We hate school."

Whump!

A muffled, kicking sound emanated from the coffin.

"What was that?" the older boy asked, his eyes opening wide.

"It's my brother," Soapy said, bowing his head in respect, and pointing to the coffin. "He passed on two days ago, rest his soul."

"He don't sound all that dead to me," the older boy said, scrutinizing the coffin with curious eyes.

Whump!

Both boys jumped when the thud sounded from the coffin.

Soapy groaned, climbed down from Devil, and jumped up into the wagon.

He rapped on the coffin several times. "Oh, he is, boys. He is as dead as an empty can of beans."

Soapy wiped a tear from his eyes and focused on the older boy. "When he was alive, Carl—that was his name, Carl—was the laziest man in three states and four Canadian provinces. He would hardly even move, except to eat and drink, he was so lazy. He never went to school, either. He was the world's laziest man."

Soapy nodded toward the boys. "He's making up for it now, I reckon."

Whump!

Both boys jumped again. Soapy was sure he saw them begin to shake a little.

"What do you mean, making up for it now?" the older boy asked.

"It's called spontaneous, combustulated, reactivated, anti-laziness syndrome," Soapy said. "Happens all the time. I'd be glad to let you have a look, if you want. It's a sight to see! His eyeballs will be poking in and out, his big old bloated hands will be shaking, and his legs will kick back and forth, as if a big old skeeter bug was biting the daylights out of them!"

Soapy wiped another tear from his eyes. "It would be funny, except poor ol' Carl is as dead as a sixteen-penny coffin nail."

Both boys had scooted back several paces by now.

"Say!" Soapy grabbed the lid of the coffin. "Don't you guys want to look? Don't run home and tell your mother, though. This sort of thing makes mothers pass out."

Soapy snatched the lid open and stared down at the sheriff.

"Aiiee!" he screamed, as if in anguish. "Worms! The worms have got to dear old Carl! Oh! You boys have got to see *this*!"

Soapy reached to grab the youngest boy.

"Aiiee!" both boys yelled. They took off, running down the street as fast as they could. By the time they quit running and stopped to see how far they had gone, the two mounted riders and the wagon were no longer in sight.

It took Joe, Chili, and Soapy more than three hours to go around the mountain and reach the railroad camp.

"How do you make fake tears?" Chili asked Soapy. "Like you did back there with those boys?"

"They weren't fake," Soapy said. "I *did* have a brother, Carl, and he *was* the laziest man I ever did see."

"Did he die?" Chili asked.

"Yep."

"And did he . . . jump around like you said? That spontaneous whatchamacallit?"

Soapy dramatically wiped a tear from his eyes. "Nope. Just the opposite. The dumb carpenter who made the casket, leaned Carl up against the wall of the shop when he measured him for the box. Carl got stuck in a sitting position. When they placed him in the coffin, both his legs stuck straight up in the air. It was a sight none of us ever forgot."

Chili wrinkled his brow and looked hard at Soapy. He was not sure whether the man was pulling his leg or not.

"I had a brother, too," Chili said. "He was the—"

"Enough, you two!" Joe called out, pointing to a long shed in the distance. "Just ahead is the railroad station, where the tracks from Lost Gulch come to an end, and the narrow gauge starts up the mountain. It's time to quit telling stories and go to work."

The three came to a halt and focused on the shed and tracks ahead of them. They could see where the narrow-gauge tracks snaked back and forth up the side of the mountain. The narrower tracks were used on mountains because they were less expensive to build and maintain. There were huge cuts in the forests on the side of the mountain, as well as exposed cliffs that had been dynamited out to make way for the rails.

"How far up do you suppose the mine is?" Joe asked Soapy.

"Near the top, I figure. Otherwise, they wouldn't go to the trouble of putting a rail in at all. They'd just dynamite the whole hill and wait for the gold to fall to the bottom."

"It looks as if they're only part of the way up," Joe said.

"About a sixth, I'd guess," Soapy said. "They've got a long ways to go. They're gonna need a heap of cheap prison labor to finish that one."

There were several explosions, from somewhere on the

mountain, but they could not detect smoke or dust from where they stood.

"Let's ride on," Joe said, flicking the reins to give Davey the go-ahead.

The railroad camp was dominated by a long shed, which housed materials and the locomotive. Beyond the shed were six canvas tents and eight boxcars. Four of the boxcars were situated away from the others, behind a six-foot wooden stockade.

"You think that's where the prisoners are kept?" Chili asked Soapy. "In those awful boxcars behind the fence?"

"Has to be. They can cram fifty men inside each one. The poor souls will hardly be able to breathe all night long, stacked on top of one another like a burrow filled with prairie dogs."

Soapy wiped a tear from his eyes. "I've seen this sort of set-up on the railroad before, in Nevada. Track bosses are hired to lay the tracks, and they have to finish so many feet per day. They don't give a good cigar about the men, or how they are treated at night, as long as they do the work."

Several hundred paces this side of the shed and tents, a stream emptied into a small, dammed pond, and several wagons were camped around the pond.

"Let's give the horses a drink," Joe said. "That'll give us time to plan."

As the horses drank from the cool, clear water, Joe scanned the wagons, and thought one looked more familiar than the others.

"Isn't that Micah's wagon?" he asked Soapy. "You remember—the family we helped with the wheel outside of Idaho Springs?"

"Looks like it," Soapy said.

Smoke billowed up from a camp fire on the other side of the wagon, and Joe walked over to have a better look.

"Micah!" he called out when he recognized the homesteader, who sat with his wife and son as they prepared their noon meal.

"Joe!" Micah replied, jumping up. The two men clasped hands.

"I figured you'd be half way through the Divide by now," Joe said.

"Nope. I finally convinced the Missus to stop before winter set in. I hired on here, as a tree cutter, but that only lasted a day or so. We would chop down cottonwoods to be used as railroad ties." He narrowed his eyes. "These men use prisoners to do most of their dirty work, Joe. It is not a good situation. They are cruelly mistreated."

"That's what I've heard," Joe said.

Micah grinned broadly. "But we have plenty of food, Joe. Won't you join us?"

"No, thanks, Micah. I'm with two other men. We're still looking for my friend, Tommy."

Micah slapped Joe on the shoulder. "We have enough food for three, Joe. I insist you join us. Besides, I have something of importance to tell you."

"You do? What?"

"This young boy you seek? Tommy?"

"Yes? You have news of him?"

"Indeed I do, Joe." Micah nodded somberly. "Tommy is here. He works for the railroad bosses."

"Thank goodness! We've found him! Now I can get him and we can head out for home!"

Micah shook his head. "It won't be that easy, Joe. Tommy doesn't work voluntarily. He is not being paid wages. He is, to put it one way, chained to his job. Tommy is a slave."

Chapter Eighteen

Micah and his family welcomed Joe, Soapy, and Chili with open arms. Micah's wife had prepared pan-fried, fresh mountain trout and cornbread.

Soapy ate three helpings of cornbread before he even started on the fish. Chili was sure that he saw real tears run down the man's face while he chewed merrily away.

"My son, Jake, caught the fish this morning," Micah said proudly. "He is becoming a first-class fisherman, even though he is only six."

Jake beamed under his father's doting words.

"Tell me more about Tommy," Joe said, savoring the delicious, flaky fish. "Is he nearby? Can I see him? Can I reach him to talk to him?"

"You can *see* him, later. But I doubt you will be able to get close enough to him to trade words."

"Why not? What's he do?"

"He works on the hand-pump car."

"The hand-pump car? What's that?"

Micah pointed toward the narrow gauge track. "See that bumper? The large, wooden structure at the end of the rail?"

Joe nodded.

"The bumper is to stop the pump car if the brakes fail. The car has a hand pump, and four men are usually used to pump it up and down, to move it along the tracks. This one is driven by four young boys, Tommy included. They are expected to pump the car up the mountain, using nothing but their physical strength. When they come downhill, they must use the brakes to slow the car down. The bumper is in case the brakes burn up. The reason they use the young boys is because they are expendable. I was told by the other loggers that the hand car brakes fail once or twice every month."

"But if they crash into the bumper, won't they be hurt?" Joe asked. "It doesn't look like a soft stop."

"It's not. When an out-of-control pump car hits the bumper, all aboard usually perish. The purpose of the bumper is not to protect the riders of the hand car, but to protect the tents beyond."

Joe mused in silence. The situation did not sound good. "I still find it difficult to believe," he said, "that four boys can pump a car up the mountain. It seems impossible."

"It's not impossible," Micah said, "just very difficult. They must pump it up, and come back down, two times a day. It is their job to take dinner and supper to the workers.

Sometimes a rail boss will ride with them, whipping them for going too slowly. It is very sad to watch, Joe."

Joe clenched his fists and rose. "I've heard enough," he said. "It's time to act. The longer we wait, the greater the chances of the pump car wrecking."

"I have one more item that may be of interest to you, Joe," Micah said, standing up beside him. "The men who stole the cattle and horses from your ranch are here, as well."

"What? Where?"

Micah pointed to a corral on the other side of the tents. "Your stock are in the corral, over there. Those rustlers work for the railroad. It's their job to bring in fresh beef and other provisions for the workers."

Joe grimaced. "Thanks, Micah. We appreciate your information. But now, it's time for the three of us to go to work. You and your family need to remain here. You stay out of this, for your own safety."

Micah's wife suddenly stood up. "We are *not* staying out of this, Joe!"

Joe was flabbergasted. He had never heard the woman speak.

"These are *horrible* men, and we have remained here for one purpose only. We knew you would be coming and we searched out information, so we could pass it on when you arrived. We are going to help you."

She shot Joe a genuine smile.

"We cannot stand by and allow injustice to take place."

"Sarah is right," Micah added. "We have discussed this.

That could be our son on that pump car. We are going to help you, Joe, and then we are going to leave this forsaken place."

"You said the pump car goes up and down twice a day?" Joe asked Micah, who nodded.

"When will it be back at the bottom again?"

"Soon," Micah said. "They should have made the noon run by now, and shortly will be on their way down. They never run on time, however. It is too strenuous. That's why the rail bosses beat the boys. They take the blame for being late, even though four strong *men* could not pump that car up the mountain much faster."

"How close can we get to the car?" Joe asked.

"You can go right up to it. There are strangers passing through here all the time, so the guards are used to it. But they won't let you close enough to get on or to talk to the boys. They don't want *anyone* to ask the boys what they are doing."

"Where is the rail boss?" Joe asked.

"His name is Campion. He's called Boss Campion. He stays in a caboose that's pushed up the incline early every morning by the narrow gauge engine. The engine pulls two flat cars at the same time with the workers on it."

"How are new prisoners transported up to the work? What if they are brought in during the day? Is there any chance they are taken up on the pump car?"

"Not really. They would normally be taken to one of the boxcars in the prisoners' compound. Then, the next day, they would go up on one of the flat cars, under heavy guard. There is not enough strength in the boys to take prisoners up on the small car."

"We'll try it, anyway," Joe said. "It's the only way I can see to get to Tommy without trying to grab him from under the watchful eyes of ten guards."

"There are close to fifty guards," Micah said. "They're everywhere."

"How many workers are there?" Joe asked. "Prison workers?"

"Over two hundred."

"That's about one guard for every four prisoners. It seems like a waste of manpower."

"Until you realize that the prisoners are not paid, nor fed, for that matter. All they get to eat is beans and rice. Not much else. They're probably all chomping at the bit to escape from this forsaken place."

Joe stood, deep in thought for several moments. "Okay," he said. "I have a plan."

The three men, Sarah, and Jake all crowded close to him.

"We'll take Sheriff Matterson out of the casket—"

"A dead man?" Jake asked.

"Shh, Jake!" Sarah scolded. "Be quiet and listen!"

"We'll take him out," Joe continued, "and lead him up to the pump car, as if he's a prisoner. I'll be wearing his badge. I'll pretend I'm a deputy, and we need to transport him to the rail boss at once, as if it's an emergency. Soapy, you'll come with me. And be sure to bring the last of your black powder, too."

"Do you need explosives?" Micah asked. "I have some."

"You do?" Joe asked. "Yes. We can use all we can come across."

Micah went to the wagon and brought back five sticks of dynamite, with blasting caps attached, and fifty feet of fuse. He set them down in front of Soapy. "I picked these up from a Chinese man in Denver. He said he was a powder man and this fuse was the best made."

Soapy looked over the fuse and the dynamite. "Did he tell you the timing on the fuse? It sure is a long one."

"He said it was for special occasions," Micah said. "He called it 'fast and in plain sight,' whatever that means."

Soapy grinned even wider. "A powder man term," he said. "I know what it means, and it might just be perfect for what we need. The Chinese make the best fuses available. Thanks, Micah."

"How about me, Joe?" Chili asked. "What am I to do?"

"You stay here with Micah, Chili. Actually, your jobs are more dangerous. First, have all our mounts fed, watered, and ready to ride. Then, I want you two to go to the corral, round up our stock, and have them ready to ride out of here when we return."

Joe looked at Micah. "How many guards will there be on the corral?"

"About five. No more. The rest are needed to keep an eye on the prisoners. There will be two at the boxcars, watching sick and hurt men, two at the bumper, and the rest will be on the mountain, about forty of them."

"What do the corral guards do for their noon meal?" Chili asked.

"Sometimes, women from the wagons, here, will take them food. They pay pretty good money for good food."

Chili grinned. "Señora Sarah? If you will assist me, we will give the corral guards a meal they will not soon forget!"

"I'll be glad to help," Sarah said.

"Me, too!" Jake piped in. "What can I do?"

"You'll be the lookout, Jake," Joe said, knowing how badly the boy wanted to help them. "It'll be your job to let Chili know if anything looks suspicious."

"I'm not sure what you have got in mind for us, Joe," Soapy said. "But I do see one problem, so far."

"What's that?"

"The sheriff. What if he talks? We can't keep him gagged the whole time. Sooner or later, someone will take it off. When that happens, our gooses are cooked."

"I have an answer to that little problem, too," Chili said. "I can cook the goose better than *anyone*!"

"What can you do, Chili?" Joe asked.

"Is it time?" Chili asked. "Are we ready to go to work?"

Joe nodded. His plan was not worked out in very much detail, but he knew they had to start somewhere, and they could not wait forever.

"It's time," he said.

Without another word, Chili walked over to their wagon. The others followed close behind. He patted Cortabolsas gently, and jumped up into the wagon, next to the coffin.

"My magic sombrero," Chili said to those watching him below. He snatched off his hat and opened the coffin. He pulled one of his paper packets out of the sweat band, checked to be sure it was opened, and pulled the gag off Sheriff Matterson's mouth.

"You fellers are in *big* trouble, now!" the sheriff yelled. "When I get—"

Chili poured the contents of the envelope in the sheriff's mouth while the man was yelling.

"—out of here, you varmints will wish . . . Ahh! Uhh! Ah can't ahh! What ith thith?"

Within several seconds, the sheriff was unable to speak. He opened his mouth, but no sound came out.

"What did you give him?" Micah asked. "A magic potion?"

"Nope," Chili replied. "I doused his vocal chords with pure, home-grown jalapeño chiles. He won't be able to talk for days!"

Chapter Nineteen

Joe and Chili drove the wagon carrying Sheriff Matterson and the dynamite up to the bumper at the end of the narrow gauge rail line. They were immediately accosted by two armed guards. The guards did not pull their guns, but eyed the two with suspicion.

"What can we do for you cowpokes?" the taller guard said.

"We've got a prisoner," Joe replied, smiling at the guard as he climbed down. He angled his head at Matterson, tied up in the back of the wagon. "Need to take him to Boss Campion. We're supposed to go up to the top of the rail, pronto."

The taller guard eyed Joe's badge. "I haven't seen you before. You work for Sheriff . . . uh, Jackson?"

"Never heard of Sheriff Jackson," Joe said, realizing the guard was trying to trick him. "We work for Sheriff Matterson, the best, and the meanest, durn sheriff in the entire state."

Joe winked at Sheriff Matterson as he said the kind words about him to the guard.

"Uhh!" Sheriff Matterson muttered. "Ah uh shruff! Ahh mmm!"

"What's wrong with him?" the shorter guard asked. "Cat got his tongue?"

Both guards laughed at the joke.

"We think he's got smallpox," Joe said, trying hard to think of the most terrible disease he could. "That's why we need to see the Boss. Any prisoners brought up from Idaho Springs in the last two weeks might be infected."

Both guards took several steps backwards, away from the wagon.

"Smallpox?" the taller one asked. "Are you sure?"

"No," Joe said, truthfully. "But it *might* be the smallpox. That's why we need to see Boss Campion and get him to find a doctor to make a professional diagnosis."

"Here they come!" the shorter guard yelled. "The pump car. You fellers can leave, now. Those boys will be tired, but like you said, this is an emergency. You might have to beat 'em a bit, to make 'em pump it up the hill so soon after coming down."

"No problem," Joe said, eyeing the short guard intensely. He wanted to make sure he would not forget this man for his remark.

With an ear-splitting screech of steel on steel, the pump car braked its way down the slope toward the bumper. Joe watched in horror, as the car, going much faster than he thought it should be traveling, lurched down the rail, sparks spurting from beneath its wheels. Even with the brakes applied as hard as the boys could manage, the car slammed into the wooden bumper.

Wham!

All four of the boys on the car were yanked back and forth. Only the chains kept them from being thrown off the pump car.

Joe sighed with relief when he saw all four young men climb to their feet, then slump back down onto the bed of the car, completely exhausted. At least they were not seriously hurt. He glanced with dismay at Tommy. He was emaciated, and his bare back revealed the many welts from lashes he had received from these vermin.

Joe's eyes met Tommy's for a split second. Tommy immediately glanced in another direction, so the guards would not suspect anything. In that second, Joe could see the hope well up in Tommy's tired, blood-shot eyes.

"Get on your feet, you lazy dirt clods!" the taller guard yelled, punching two of the boys until they stood up. "Got to make an emergency run, up to the top again. You can rest once you come back down. Get up, I said!"

Reluctantly, as if under a spell, the four boys grabbed the handles to the pump mechanism. As soon as Soapy loaded the bag and Joe pulled Sheriff Matterson on board, the boys began pumping on the handles of the pump car.

"You need to beat 'em!" the short guard yelled. "Those boys are as lazy as cold molasses. You've got to whip 'em if you want to make the top before sundown!"

"Pump faster," Joe yelled at the boys, "or I'll knock the stuffing out of you!"

The three boys not in on the ruse began pumping for all they were worth. Tommy, who had an idea what was going on, pumped just as hard. He did not want the guards to become suspicious.

As soon as the car had moved up the incline and around the bend about two hundred paces, it reached a level grade and Joe called out for them to stop.

Soapy opened the bag and took out a hammer and a cold chisel. He went to work on the chains and in several minutes had cut all four of the boys loose.

Joe and Tommy hugged each other, silently, as the other three boys watched with wonder. They had no idea what was going on.

"Don't have time to explain right now," Joe told them. "Just do as you're told, and we'll fill you in as soon as we can."

He chained Sheriff Matterson to one of the pump handles, then grabbed the other side of the bar. "Time to earn your keep, Sheriff!" Joe yelled at him. "You pump, or I'll have Soapy put a lit stick of dynamite down your shorts and throw you off!"

The sheriff got the message and pumped as hard as he could. Soapy grabbed the other side of the pump, and together, the three men worked the pump car up the mountain. The four boys watched in wonder.

"Why are we going *up*, Joe?" Tommy asked. He had collapsed on his side, supporting his head with one arm. "Why don't we *leave* this place? Now!"

Joe continued to pump as he explained the situation to Tommy.

"We can't leave, yet, Tommy. I won't leave until every prisoner here is a free man. Once we can say for sure that they are all free, then we can leave."

Tommy slumped down even more than he had been.

"I don't think you can do that, Joe," he said. "I've watched these vermin for too long. I've been with them for too long. Nothing can defeat them. There's too many of them. What you want to do, is . . . impossible."

While Joe, Soapy, and Sheriff Matterson pumped the hand car, Joe talked with Tommy and the other three boys, Jim, Keith, and Bob. Joe explained that all four boys were an integral part of his plan, and they all agreed to help.

"Once we get to the caboose," Joe said, "you guys have to stay with the pump car, as if you're still chained to it. I realize it might be tempting to cut and run, but for our plan to be successful, you have to remain at your post. Can you guys do that?"

"Yes!" all four said at once.

"Tommy, you need to warn me before we reach the caboose," Joe said. "We have some preparatory work to do, while we are out of sight of the guards."

"I've got you, Joe," Tommy said. "I know this grade like the back of my hand. I can tell you every level spot, every turn, and every dip and rise."

"I know you do, Tommy. You learned it the hard way, now let's *use* what you learned against these outlaws."

"Umm tahd!" Sheriff Matterson tried to yell.

"What was that?" Joe asked. "You're tired?"

The sheriff nodded.

"Let go of the handle, Soapy," Joe said, dropping his own hands off the pump handle. "Let's let Sheriff Matterson take it the rest of the way by himself."

"Uhn! Uhn cnnt!" the sheriff mumbled.

"Tommy? Do you suppose you, Keith, Jim, and Bob can convince the sheriff to work harder?"

The four boys grinned and moved in on the sheriff, who did not utter another sound as he furiously pumped the car up the mountainside.

"We're close!" Tommy told Joe, as they rounded a curve. "The caboose and the workers are beyond this curve, several hundred paces away."

Joe made the sheriff quit pumping and pulled him off the car. He took the sheriff into the nearby woods, out of sight of any curious eyes, and re-chained him around a huge cedar tree trunk.

"I hope we don't forget to come and get you, Sheriff. I hope we don't leave you up here like this. But if we do, you have a nice winter."

Joe got back on the car and had the boys finish pumping the car from that point on, so that no one who saw them would be suspicious.

"Slow it down," Joe said, as they came within sight of the caboose. "Let me study the lay of the land. We have to stop in the right place for our plan to work."

The car slowed, and Joe and Soapy scanned the ground ahead.

"Right there!" Soapy said, pointing to an area on the tracks about twenty paces forward.

The boys quit pumping at that spot and Joe studied the sight. The track made a gentle curve to the right, and the caboose was about a hundred paces ahead. The track was built up on a high gravel bed, and directly to their right, the ground sloped downhill about ten feet, then began rising to form a hill fifty feet high.

"Will this do?" Joe asked Soapy. "The ravine is about ten feet deep. How about the hill? Will it work for us?"

"It's perfect, Joe. It's a man-made hill, built out of rubble. It will suit us to a tee."

Soapy grabbed the bag containing the fuse and the dynamite, and jumped off the car. He went down the ravine, then began climbing the hill above.

"We need to park the car here," Joe told the boys. "Don't let anyone make you move it. If they try, tell them the brakes are locked up, and you're waiting for an engine mechanic. I'll be back as soon as I can. Just try to remain calm and act normal."

Before Joe could jump down, Tommy grabbed him and hugged him tightly.

"I knew you'd come for me, Joe. I knew it. Thanks. And I'm sorry I had doubts about your plan. It'll work. I'm positive it'll work just great!"

"It might not," Joe said, trying to be realistic. "But we've got to try it. We can't just leave this place when there are men in the same situation as you guys were in."

"I know, Joe. Good luck! Go get 'em!"

Joe left the car and walked the hundred paces to the caboose, which was much more elegant than he had thought it might be.

Painted a bright red, the caboose looked more like a hotel on wheels than a train car. It had glass windows all the way down both sides, shaded with canvas awnings. On the roof was an elegant handrail all the way around, and there were several chairs and sun parasols, giving the roof the look of a mansion balcony.

Four guards, all armed with rifles, stood at the corners of the caboose. Joe hoped that Teton Tom, Hoosegow, and Beans were not in the vicinity, and would not see him.

Several hundred paces beyond the fancy railroad car, Joe could see the men working on the rails. They were busy digging, breaking up rocks with hammers and picks, unloading gravel, setting ties, and placing steel rails on the finished beds. The entire time Joe watched, the workers were yelled at and beaten with bull whips to prod them on. Joe's stomach knotted as he watched the terrible mistreatment of the workers.

Joe was more determined than ever to carry out his plans.

He walked up to the caboose as if getting inside were no problem, but two of the guards jumped in his path.

"What do you want?" one of them asked.

"Got to see Boss Campion," Joe said. "I have an urgent message from Sheriff Matterson in Idaho Springs."

"Wait here," the guard said. He ran up the steps and into the caboose.

A few moments later, the guard re-opened the door and stuck out his head.

"Hey, you!" he called out. "The Boss will see you. Leave your weapon with Bill."

Joe handed his revolver to the guard next to him, and walked up the steps into the caboose. The guard who had called for him kept his rifle on Joe the whole time.

Joe was impressed. The outside of the caboose was nice, but the interior of the car was furnished better than any home or hotel he had ever been in. The walls were paneled with thick slabs of dark mahogany, the ceiling was made from hammered copper plate, and the floor was covered with wall-to-wall sheepskin. There were shades drawn over the windows, cutting out most of the sunlight, casting dark shadows through the room. It was difficult for Joe to see, and he squinted his eyes.

The furniture consisted of two over-stuffed couches, and four huge, leather chairs, placed around a four-foot-wide, six-foot-long, six-inch-thick oak table.

Two of the chairs were occupied. In one was a large man, over two hundred pounds, seated at the far end of the table. Joe recognized him—it was Teton Tom. Joe pulled his hat down over his eyes, and tried to keep his face turned away. He was glad the room was so dark, and as far as he could tell, Teton Tom showed no signs of recognition.

The other man, sitting near Joe, was smaller, only about 5'4" tall, with long, black hair, carefully swept back away from his eyes and behind his ears. He had thin, constantly moving fingers, that drummed on the table top the entire time Joe was in the room.

Joe guessed that this man was Boss Campion. His steel-gray eyes never left Joe's for an instant. Joe felt that the man's cold, steel demeanor probably went straight through to his heart.

"Well?" Boss Campion said to Joe, in a high, nasal twang. "What do you want? You wear a sheriff's badge, but I don't know you."

"I'm a new deputy," Joe said, fingering the tin badge. "I work for Sheriff Matterson, and we're out of deputy's badges, so he lent me this one. He sent me up here to get you. He said to tell you it was urgent. He wants you to come down to the shed at the bottom of the rail line, as soon as possible."

Boss Campion fixed Joe with hard, unblinking eyes. "You're a liar." He turned to the guard. "Take this liar outside and shoot him."

Chapter Twenty

"Wait!" Joe called out. He had never thought faster in his life. "What do you mean, calling me a liar? I was sent here by the sheriff, and I suggest you do as he asks. If you don't, you not only jeopardize his life, *you* are in trouble, too!"

"How is *that* so?" Boss Campion asked, raising his hand to stop the guard.

"That's why the sheriff couldn't come in person," Joe said. "He's in trouble! That's why he sent me."

"Who *are* you?" Boss Campion asked. "I've never seen you before."

"I'm Ben Stephens," Joe said. "I'm Deputy Wallace's brother-in-law. He's married to my sister, Julie." Joe hoped that Boss Campion did not know Deputy Wallace well enough to know his wife's name, because he was making all of this up.

170

Boss Campion scratched his chin. "Why didn't Wallace come, instead of you?"

"He was needed at the jail. Because of the Army."

"The Army? How? Colonel Andrews is one of *my* men. We don't have any problems with the Army."

"You do now," Joe said.

Having been a scout with the Army throughout Kansas and Colorado for several years, Joe knew who Colonel Andrews was. He always had figured the man to be a crook. His suspicions were correct.

"Colonel Andrews got called back to Fort Hays, in Kansas," Joe said. "He's been replaced by Colonel Bartholomew, who's down at the bottom of the rail with Sheriff Matterson. There's a company of soldiers in Idaho Springs, with Wallace. That's why my brother-in-law stayed in town, and why I'm here. Sheriff Matterson couldn't come up the rail, because the new colonel said he wasn't riding a flimsy hand-pump car anywhere, up or down a rail line."

Boss Campion laughed and slapped his thighs. "Now I get it. Why didn't you say all this to begin with?" He glanced at Teton Tom.

"Come on, Teton. Let's go talk business with the new Army colonel. I'm sure that we have enough gold to convince him to turn a blind eye to our little operation."

The two men rose, and Joe began to think his plan might work after all.

"Lead the way, Deputy," Boss Campion said, and the two men, along with two guards, followed Joe down to the hand-pump car.

Joe stopped them all once they reached the ravine below the car. "Wait here," he said. "I'll have to get rid of that old guy on the car, to make room for us. It'll just take a second."

Soapy sat on the edge of the car, puffing happily on a cigar, as the four boys stared down at Joe and the others with fear in their eyes.

Joe climbed up the ravine and got on the car. When he turned to look down on Boss Campion, Teton, and the two guards, all four had their weapons pointed at him.

"What's wrong?" Joe asked.

"That's what *I* want to know," Boss Campion said. "My partner, Teton Tom, says that he thinks he knows you, Mister Deputy Sheriff. He thinks he's seen you some place, and it wasn't in Idaho Springs. Something's fishy here, and I want to know why. Come on down here, Mister Deputy Sheriff, and let us have a better look at your face."

"Hey, fellers!" Soapy called out, waving his cigar at the men in the ravine.

"Hey, yourself, old-timer," Boss Campion called back. "Get your hands in the air. Do you work for me? I don't recognize you."

"I'm fixing to go on the payroll in just a minute," Soapy said. "Full time. I'm a powder man."

"We don't need any more powder men," Boss Campion said. "We've got a full crew."

"You ain't got any as good as me, Boss. Watch this! Have you fellers ever seen the type of fuse the Chinese call 'fast and in plain sight'? It's a pure wonder, fellers. It'll shoot by you so fast, your eyes will burn!" Soapy touched the fuse dangling in front of him with the cigar.

All eyes followed the streaking line of fire as it ran down from the pump car, past the four men, then up the hill behind them.

Boss Campion yelled at Soapy. "What in—"

Ka-blam!

It was too late. Before Boss Campion could finish his sentence, the dynamite Soapy had buried at the top of the hill exploded, sending several tons of loose rock and dirt into the ravine where Boss Campion, Teton Tom, and the two guards stood, frozen in shock.

The avalanche happened so fast that none of the men were able to move out of the way. Boss Campion and one of the guards were buried in rock and debris up to their necks, and Teton Tom and the other guard were covered up to their shoulders.

Joe signaled to the boys, and all four immediately took off, running up the hill past the caboose.

Joe jumped down and walked over to Boss Campion, where he knelt down to talk to the man.

Suddenly, an armed contingent of Boss Campion's guards, about twenty men, came running up to the top of the hill above them, where they stopped when they saw Joe standing next to four heads buried in rock.

"Stop right there and drop your guns!" Joe called out to them. He pulled his own revolver and pointed the barrel at Boss Campion.

"You men drop your weapons and surrender, or Boss Campion dies. Do as I say, and do it *now*!"

None of the men made the slightest move to do as Joe had commanded.

"They don't believe you," Boss Campion said. "They don't really think you'll shoot me. Neither do I."

"You're probably right, Boss," Soapy said, as he sidled up to Joe and the four heads. He dropped a stick of dynamite on the ground, and it rolled up under Boss Campion's chin. The fuse was about five feet long, and Soapy held it in one hand, about two inches away from the cigar he held in his other hand.

"But, you know, Boss, some people say we powder men are a little crazy. This wouldn't be the first time I lit a stick of dynamite right under my very own nose." Soapy waved the stubs of his missing fingers at Boss Campion.

"This fuse may look good and long, but it's another one of those Chinese 'fast and in plain sight' types. If I light this end, accidentally or on purpose, it doesn't matter, it'll only take about three seconds to hit the dynamite." Soapy inched the cigar closer to the fuse. "I'll sure as tarnation light you up, Boss Campion, if those men don't drop their weapons."

"Drop your guns!" Boss Campion yelled as loud as he could. "Drop your guns and do what he says!"

This time, all of the armed guards did as they were told. At the same time, the four boys came running up to the top of the hill, with almost all of the railroad prisoners right behind. The prisoners picked up the dropped weapons and held them on the former guards.

Joe and Soapy climbed up to the hand car and were joined by Tommy and the other three boys.

"You men are free now!" Joe yelled to the assembled workmen. "Can you watch over these crooks until I can send the U.S. marshal?"

"You bet we can!" several of the men yelled back.

"My advice is to leave these four right where they are!" Joe called out. "And lock up the others in a boxcar. Does that sound good to you men?"

"Sure does!" most of them yelled back to Joe.

One man slid down the hill and came to a stop in front of Boss Campion. He pulled a pigeon feather out of his pocket and began tickling Boss Campion's nose with it, causing him to sneeze violently.

"Ha!" the man shouted to Joe. "You take your time finding the marshal. I'm going to tickle these varmints so much over the next few days, they won't ever laugh again!"

"You keep that dynamite right where I dropped it!" Soapy yelled to the man. "It'll give them something to look at, and to think about, until the law gets here."

Joe, Soapy, and the boys waved good-bye to the crowd and began their journey back down the rail. There were two hand brakes, one for each front wheel, and Joe worked one, while Soapy worked the other.

About halfway down, Soapy yelled.

"Joe! Joe! I think we've got a little problem!"

"What is it?" Joe asked.

"The doggone brake! It doesn't seem to be working like it should!"

Tommy jumped over to the hand brake and tried it for himself.

"He's right, Joe!" Tommy yelled. "The brake's burned through!"

"What'll we do?" Soapy yelled.

"Only two things possible!" Tommy answered. "We can jump and hope we only break an arm or a leg. But, most likely, we'll crack our heads wide open."

"What's the other thing?" Soapy asked.

"We can let it hit the bumper and hope we only break an arm or a leg!"

"Don't jump!" Joe yelled. "We're going too fast. There's nothing but rock and gravel beds on both sides. We'll never make it if we jump."

"We'll never make it if we *don't* jump!" Soapy yelled.

"Give me a chance to think!" Joe said. "Keep trying your brake, Soapy, and I'll stay on this one. Even one brake will slow us down some."

Soapy and Joe pushed on the brake levers as hard as they could. Joe could see hot sparks trail off behind the wheel he was braking. Behind Soapy's wheel there were no sparks.

"We're almost to the bottom, Joe!" Tommy called out. "We go around this bend, and then the track levels out for about three-hundred paces. At the end of that is the bumper!"

The hand car flew around the curve, and suddenly the huge, solid-wood bumper was within their sight.

"What in blazes is that?" Joe yelled, pointing toward the end of the rail.

The car whizzed forward, barely slowing, even though Joe was pushing on his brake lever with everything he had.

"It looks like . . . hay!" Soapy yelled.

"Hay?" Joe and the four boys shouted at the same time.

"Yah-hoo!" Soapy called out. "Someone has planned ahead for our *fast* return. There's *hay* scattered all over the tracks. There seems to be loose hay, baled hay, and even hay stacks! We've got a chance, Joe! It's slim, but we've got a chance!"

"Hold on tight, everyone!" Joe yelled. "We'll make it! Don't give up!"

The car smashed through the first bale of hay, and Joe could swear that the swiftly traveling vehicle did, in fact, slow down.

Then it ran through loose hay, two more bales of hay, more loose hay, and finally, four huge stacks of hay.

With a gentle thud, the hand car came to a rest at the bumper.

Not a single one of them was even thrown overboard.

Chapter Twenty-one

"**W**elcome back, amigos!" Chili yelled, as he, Micah, Sarah, and Jake ran up to the pump car and greeted the frightened crew.

"We wanted to make sure you arrived safely," Chili said, "so we decided to welcome you with a big *hay!*"

"Hay to *you,*" Joe said, laughing. "What made you decide to put the hay on the tracks to slow us down, Chili? That was a wonderful idea."

Joe jumped down and clasped Chili's hand, thanking him again.

"It was all Chili's idea," Micah said. "He told us that you were a cowboy, not a railroad man, and then reminded us that the pump car was old and rusty. He said that putting the hay on the tracks wouldn't hurt any if the pump car's brakes *did* work, and it might come in handy if they *didn't* work. We agreed, so all of us chipped in to help him cover the tracks in hay."

"It's a good thing, too," Joe said. "We were thinking about jumping, and if we had, we probably wouldn't have all made it." He glanced around, as if expecting something else to happen.

"Where are . . . the guards?" Joe asked. "I thought they might be here to give us some trouble."

"Don't worry about the guards," Jake said. "Chili and El Gato took care of them!"

"El Gato?" Tommy asked. "I sure missed that big, ugly lizard."

"He may be ugly," Jake said, "but he sure was helpful. Chili went up to each guard, one at a time, and asked him to have a close look at the baby he found out in the bushes." Jake began laughing so hard, he could barely finish telling the story.

"Chili had El Gato wrapped up in a shawl, and when the guard would peek at him, he snapped!"

"It is very difficult," Chili added, while Jake bent over laughing, "for a man to draw his revolver with a three-foot reptile clinging to his nose with jaws that won't let go."

"After Chili subdued each of the guards," Micah said, "we locked them all in a boxcar. We released the prisoners who were locked up, the ones on night shift who were asleep, and they are now the guards of the outlaw guards."

"Did the prisoners understand what we were doing?" Joe asked. "Are they on our side?"

"The former prisoners," Chili said, "are happier than a Gila monster with a tummy full of eggs. Those men will keep the bad guys locked up until the law shows up."

Chili glanced toward Micah, Sarah, and Jake, then turned to Joe. "One more little thing, Joe."

"Oh? What?"

"I asked Micah and his family to winter over with us at the Summerlin ranch. Micah and Jake are pretty good cowboys. They can help us take the herd back down, and Sarah's a good cook. She can help me in the kitchen. They're willing to work, so it's not as if they're staying for free. I didn't think Missus Summerlin would mind. Do you?"

"Not after all the help they've been, Chili. I'm sure Missus Summerlin will be more than happy to have them with us this winter."

Joe glanced toward Sarah, who was talking to the three boys who had recently been chained to the hand-pump car.

"Everything okay, Sarah?" he asked.

"Oh, yes, Joe. I was just making arrangements to get these young men returned to their families."

"Thanks, Sarah. I appreciate your help."

He looked at Chili. "How about the stock? Are we about ready to move 'em out?"

"Yes," Chili answered. "We've got Davey and Devil saddled up for you and Soapy; Cortabolsas is hitched to the wagon; and we have two of Missus Summerlin's stolen horses saddled for Micah and Tommy. Do you think that the four of you, on horseback, will be able to handle the herd?"

"I don't know," Joe said. "I'd rather have a couple more riders."

"Don't need 'em," Soapy said. "Where's Devil?"

Chili had Jake get Soapy's Shetland pony and bring her to them. Soapy spoke a few words in the spirited pony's ear, and mounted up.

"Where's the herd?" Soapy asked, trying to keep Devil calm. The little pony kicked and jumped, anxious to move around.

"In the corral," Chili answered. Soapy pointed Devil to the corral, and they took off, going much faster than Joe would have thought possible.

Chili looked at Joe. "Are we ready to move 'em out?"

"No need to wait," Joe said. "But I'm still worried that there aren't enough of us to handle a herd of cattle and horses this big."

Joe, Micah, and Tommy mounted their horses. Just before they rode off, Joe glanced toward the corral. He could hear the dull thunder of hooves.

Suddenly, at the crest of the hill, the entire herd of cattle appeared. At first Joe was frightened that it was a stampede, but as he watched, the cattle came over the top and down the hill in as orderly a fashion as he had ever witnessed.

Joe soon saw that Soapy was right when he praised Devil for being an excellent cow pony. Without so much as a spoken word from Soapy, the pony darted back and forth, circled the herd, and headed off strays before they could get more than ten paces away. The little pony would even go so far as to nip the haunches of laggard cattle, to make them catch up with the rest of the herd.

"Come on, Tommy! Come on, Micah!" Joe yelled, laughing at Devil's antics. "We've got a herd to move out! Let's go help Devil. Get up, Davey! Let's go!"

It took them four days to make the trip home, and by the time they reached the ranch, Tommy was beginning to look and act like his old self. He was still a little thin, but he ate well enough on the journey to bring a healthy glow back to his face.

The first thing they did, when the group rode into the open area in front of the ranch house, was call out for Emma and Mrs. Summerlin.

With screams of joy, the two women hugged Tommy so much, he became embarrassed at all the attention.

After they stockaded the animals, Joe made it a point to avoid Emma, who seemed to be trying to avoid him as well. It was obvious to him that Emma still blamed him that Tommy had been kidnapped.

Joe asked Micah and Jake to identify any branded horses and cattle that belonged to other ranches, and keep a list of the animals, so they could be returned to their rightful owners as soon as possible.

Not only was Mrs. Summerlin happy to get Tommy home, she was also pleased to have the extra help for the winter, and she declared that they would have a party that night. She wanted to welcome everyone properly, and to thank them for helping to return Tommy.

Joe joined the festive crowd for the sumptuous supper of grilled beef, mashed potatoes, and refried beans prepared by Chili and Sarah, but as soon as the meal was finished he went to the kitchen. He picked up two potatoes and an apple, and headed for the barn. He cut the potatoes and apple into pieces, and gave equal parts to Davey, Devil, and Cortabolsas.

"You guys did your part," Joe told the horses. "You deserve some of the rewards, as well. You should enjoy the party, too."

"And what about you?" a voice said from the doorway, startling Joe so much he jumped.

Joe recognized the voice as Emma's, and was angry with himself for being so jumpy. He grabbed a brush and began working on Davey, brushing furiously at Davey's back.

"What do you mean?" he asked, forcing himself not to look her way.

"Shouldn't *you* be enjoying the party, too?"

"Nope. I'm just fine."

"After all," Emma said, approaching Joe, "*you* are the one who went after the kidnappers. *You're* the one who found Tommy."

"I had lots of help, Emma. I didn't do it alone."

Emma picked up a brush and joined in, brushing Davey's neck and shoulders.

"The story I keep hearing," Emma said, "from Chili and Soapy and Jake and Sarah and Micah, and even from Tommy himself . . . is that you, pretty near by yourself, did it all."

"Well, I thank them for saying that, but it's not true. They helped. *All* of them."

"Maybe they did, Joe. But can you answer one question

for me? Just one?" She stopped brushing Davey and faced Joe.

"Okay. I'll answer one question." Joe continued to brush Davey.

"Without your persistence, would Tommy have been found? You never gave up, Joe, no matter what your circumstances were. Without that kind of relentless pursuit, the kidnappers wouldn't have been brought to justice, and Tommy wouldn't be home with us right now."

"Maybe not," Joe said. "But it's still . . . my fault that Tommy was kidnapped in the first place. You told me that yourself."

"Joseph Weaver!" Emma yelled, stomping her foot. "You are a stubborn fool! I said those words only to egg you on. I was scared, Joe, that I'd never see my brother again, and I said that to force you to go look for him. I didn't say it because it was true. I *know* it wasn't your fault. At the time, there wasn't anything else I could think to say. Tommy has told us how it was entirely *his* fault, not *yours*." Emma flung the brush into a corner and placed her hands on her hips.

Joe stopped brushing and looked Emma's way. He had expected to see her smiling at him, but, instead, she had a scowl on her face.

"Yeah, that Tommy," Joe said. "He's a rambunctious little guy, isn't he?"

"I wish *you* were the rambunctious one, Joseph Weaver."

"Huh? Me? What do you mean?"

"I mean, that if you were rambunctious, you wouldn't

just stand there grinning at me and brushing Davey. Instead, you'd *kiss* me."

Suddenly, the idea of giving Davey a rubdown did not seem to Joe like the best use of his time and energy. He turned to Emma, took her in his arms, and hugged her tightly. He then proceeded to show her just how rambunctious a man he could actually be.